MAGAZINE

ISBN 978-1-944866-83-9

ISSUE

When Leza first asked me to co-edit Black Telephone with her, I said yes enthusiastically, thinking it would be a beautiful way to build a community of oddfellows, and to put my reading, thinking and editing skills to work (and to ask them to grow). And it was an opportunity to build something with a friend, to have fun and play, to amplify the work of others, to share it—to be a small part of making space for challenging or disturbing or off writing that deserves recognition and a wider audience. We are different people with different preferences and histories (a good thing!), but Leza and I both wanted to invite writers to send in the kind of work that defies classification and expectation. I had seen, in the reception of my first novel, that some of us share the same hunger for stories that are dark and difficult and experimental. Maybe we aren't used to being sold dark or difficult or experimental writing, but that doesn't mean we don't have a need for it—and it doesn't mean there aren't hundreds or thousands of writers producing it everyday, all over the world, across space and time. As long as there have been people striving to communicate what is just outside our grasp—that which continually eludes—there has been the black telephone. In the spirit of this, we wanted to give Black Telephone Magazine a shot.

We somehow managed to pull it off as the pandemic hit and our lives needed to be rearranged (and rearranged, and rearranged). We committed to paying all contributors and to making each issue as diverse as possible (in multiple senses), while still finding some common aesthetic threads. I don't know how, but we did it. It began to pay off. People sent notes and emails saying that each issue had surprised and terrified and delighted them. I guess I could have anticipated all of that. What I could not have anticipated, however, is how much all the writing we would encounter (and publish) would mean so much to me—how it would surprise and terrify and delight me and stretch my aesthetic commitments, many of them lurking silently, only halfway articulated. I had picked up the black telephone. There was no going back. I like it here. I hope you do too.

LL

She picked up the black telephone.
There was nothing
but static coming through,
but then the voices came
and sang a story,
a melody
dipped in blue...

LC

TABLE OF CONTENTS

BLACK TELEPHONE MAGAZINE ISSUE 1

CARVING OUT
MY MEMORY

L CHAN

You can make a golem out of anything corporeal, anything you can mold and sculpt. There's things that you can't lay hands on, but there's ways. The tools: a crescent moon bladed flensing knife, a meat hook the size of a man's curled finger. Each tool bears inscriptions, profane under a dozen religions, jagged strokes scratched out whalebone.

Both illegal. Black market magic, the sort you go five nodes deep on the dark web to access on forums, invoiced in bitcoin, deliverable only to PO boxes from a lax service provider. Unregistered golems are already illegal; but I already have one foot wet, so I might as well carve a golem out of the sickest, deepest memories a person has.

I have just the right ones of you.

The hook bites deep into my forearm, drawing no blood, only the tingle of neuralgia to even let me know it's there. Carvings do their work when I pull; memories stretch out like taffy. I choose a good one to start, when I was at emergency to fix my face, lip split from the thick ring I bought you for our first anniversary, eye swollen shut. I told the nurse there'd been a fight at the bar and she sniffs at me, examining the smooth, unbroken skin on my knuckles. She gets me cold cocoa from the machine in the corridor and it's the nicest thing anyone has done for me in months. Yeah, a good place to start.

The edge of the blade is not sharper than a dinner knife. Memories don't cut easy, effort brings sweat to my forehead; the knife, rending and tearing, leaving a ragged edge. There's no neat way to cut out a memory.

I lay the slab of memory on our dining table. *My* dining table. Even though you moved in, and then out, and I reclaimed my body and my space, I can't quite shake that sense of ownership. Maybe I can cut it out too. Maybe I can't. I'm going to try.

I snag another memory, this time from my belly. You remember when I found your draft emails to the folks back home who didn't know about my city life? Weaponized secrets? By the time you sent out that email two fucking years after we split, I'd already told them. I don't think you remember, because you don't give a shit. Now I don't have to remember, because I've hacked it out of me, the pain of losing a memory so exquisite that it squeezes fat tears from the corners of my eyes.

I pile memories high, unmaking you in my head by excision, making you out of every fucked up thing you've ever done, every rotten memory we have together. The memory knife doesn't break skin but I bleed all the same, except it's sawdust and shame. Cutting you out of me makes me feel more whole than before. How I wish I could scrape the stink of you from my bones, but the hook can't go that deep.

Shaking hands mold the pile into something approaching the human form. Jitters can't stop the golem from looking like you, but only coming to half my height. I figured it'd be bigger, there was so much to cut out. But you were never bigger, you just made me small.

I kiss the golem on its lips; I give it its word, its *shem*, its purpose. It goes when I ask, eschewing the door for the vents, nimble as a spider. Those hands look every bit as strong as yours. Good.

I do regret what I did. Or did not do; I wasn't strong enough you see. Not to cut every memory out, just the ones I didn't want. I'm almost in love with you again at the end. All sorts of promises are being broken today. Your folks will call; they liked me more than they liked you. But even they'll be surprised when I cry at your funeral.

MARTYR

STEPHANIE
WYTOVICH

Strangle me with sweet grass,
shove crucifixes down my throat,
I am a clenched fist refusing
baptism, the words of men
a bloodied egg on my plate.

THE CRONE CONFESSIONS

When I dream about swallowing my teeth,
I often wake up hungry. I wonder
if it has something to do
with the way the moon
watches me at night, how it
glues itself to my window,
tonguing the glass
like a hungry wolf.

Confession: on Tuesdays I crawl up
the wall a shadow
only to shove mugwort
in my eyes—

It burns the way
my thighs did
when the noose
didn't work

and

I've noticed a dying bat resting between
my shoulder blades, quiet like
the still, suffocated night. We screech
like sisters, our see-through bodies
a paper jacket, a satin sheet
covering a shapeshifter,
a hysteric-sewn hag
raging in her own filth.

Confession: on Saturdays, I fill the bathtub

full of piss
only to laugh when
I drink it—

It tastes the way
my womb did
the morning I
carved it out

yet

awake on this ceiling, I masturbate
to the sounds of cardinals,
my mattress a nest, a beaten-in
bruise, my skin a wrinkled dress
I've long since taken off.

WOMAN AS EULOGY

A murder of crows rests beneath
sleepless eyes, a visual demand for silence,
this the flock of death notes and mourning,
I come to the page as widow, the bruising
in my mouth an open invitation to my wounds:

please, swallow me whole,
digest me like the sickness I am.

I've stuffed diary pages in my bones,
these trauma bonds a book of weeping sores,
my body the first chapter to a memoir
made of ghosts. Look behind the coffins
filled with flowers, underneath the floorboard
covered in layers of whisper-worn screams:

I beg of you, read my story,
sing my pain with the choir blood of angels.

It's been six years but six minutes,
this practice of choking on typewriter keys,
of mending white dresses I'll never
get to wear, my voice a carving board
for sigils, each vocal cord stained ink,
soaked twice in half-strung hexes and rage:

I promise you, the forest ate my diamond,
devoured me whole, this poison that I am

A STORY IN THREE PARTS
CYNTHIA PELAYO

MISSING GIRL

What was she wearing?
Where was she going?
Do either really matter?
What matters is she is
All gone, silent cellphone
Getting dark, car keys
Found dangling, a spot
Of blood smeared across
Passenger window, No
Cries heard. Call in the
Morning. She'll be home
Soon, but time warbles
Missing poster picture
Fades, birthdays missed
Kisses forgotten and lovers
Abandoned, and that car
Sits rusted and weightless
Clutching onto her secrets
A seashell playing back
Recorded screams of terror
Lost hope, lost life, lost

DETECTIVE STORY

The detective story is an intellectual game
Of things once there and things rearranged
Water, books, letters, keys, a herring so red
Give the reader ample opportunity to solve
The mystery, no willful tricks, do not play
Deceptions, but let's play with the detective
Rules: No love interest. Never the perpetrator
The detective must be continually turning,
Making calculations, as Dupin says ratiocination
The crime must be solved by natural means
And there must always, always be a body

SKULL BEHIND A WALL

Sometimes you know no one is ever going to find you and sometimes you relinquish your grasp, your hold on this world. You close your eyes and you allow those silent, anguished, warm tears to roll down your cheeks because they are real and they are yours and no one and nothing can rip them away from you as you were ripped away from this world and your screams *your* screams are yours, and your memories are yours and you wish you wish you had one more time to tell them all you loved them you wish you wish you had one more time to kiss the noon day sun and you wish you wish the last scent that you smelled was not the ogre above you and you wish you wish this was not the place you would haunt for years and years before they found you, covered in burlap and no way to find you and no way to find you and you will never go home because home was years ago and home was them and all of them have died and your memory fades as they faded and you are released to your second death all because an ogre stole you away.

LILITH, MY DAUGHTER

KRISTIN CLEAVELAND

Long before she was born, I dreamed of her; my nights were haunted by a child with dark hair and black eyes that did not shine. Each time I woke and found my arms empty, I felt sorrow but also relief. I had this dream for years, until it finally came true.

My only child Lilith was dragged into this world at 1:13 p.m. on a Friday after two days of excruciating labor. I suffered agonizing bouts of contractions with no progress; my daughter fought tooth and nail against any attempts to induce labor. Finally, as my blood pressure climbed, an anaesthetist dashed in and plunged a syringe full of clear fluid into my IV tubing. "Is my baby ok?" I tried to ask, but it came out garbled. Through drooping eyelids I watched a nurse smear iodine over my grossly distended abdomen. The next thing I knew was oblivion.

When I awoke, a nurse was checking my vital signs. "Where's my baby?" I slurred through cracked lips, my tongue thick with drugged sleep.

"She's right here," the nurse answered, pointing to a tiny wheeled crib next to my bed. "Would you like to hold her?" I nodded groggily and the nurse put down her chart, picked up the baby gently and laid her in my arms. When I saw my daughter for the first time, I thought I was dreaming again. Her eyes were black, wide-open, and searching. She had thick, matted black hair and mottled red skin. The nurse shook her head. "You've got a stubborn one there," she said. "She fought us every step of the way. The surgeon had to pry her fists off the umbilical cord."

I looked into Lilith's dark eyes. She gazed back at me. She did not cry.

Lilith's birth was only one of many times she fought against her own best interests. Despite all my efforts and the subtly judgmental advice of the hospital staff, my daughter refused to nurse, nor did she take a bottle. She wouldn't even open her mouth. Lilith lost weight by the hour. The doctors wouldn't release her from the hospital; they hooked her up to an IV and shoved a feeding tube up her nose and down her throat. I cried. She didn't. She blinked at me.

I was beside myself. And alone, as some of the nurses were quick to point out. Lilith's father had come and gone from my life so quickly I barely remembered him, an ephemeral stranger I'd never even tried to contact again. I had my daughter. Nothing else mattered.

I clutched her to my chest. I looked at her desperately, terrified she would starve. "Lilith," I said, tears in my throat. "I can't live without you."

She stared back at me, her eyes wide. I offered her my breast and she immediately latched on, sucking so hard I gasped in pain. As she swallowed every drop of milk, I felt weak but exhilarated. The force of her suction increased and I realized she'd emptied my breast, so I pulled away from her mouth with some difficulty and offered her the other. Needles of pain shot through my chest as she latched on again. Lilith suckled harder, draining me dry, until the pain became unbearable. When I finally pried her away, blood spilled out of her mouth and stained her striped hospital blanket. My breast, raw and torn, bore witness to a fact I hadn't realized: my daughter had been born with teeth. I wiped her mouth with the blanket and clutched her to my throbbing chest, my body stained with blood and milk. From then on, I fed her with a bottle.

Although she rallied from her traumatic birth, Lilith was ever after an odd child. She never cried, even if she skinned her knee, fell off her bike, or worse. Once, to my horror, I found Lilith crumpled at the bottom of the stairs, her limbs twisted at odd angles. "Don't worry," she said, sounding almost disappointed. "It's only a broken bone or two." Another time, when the house lights suddenly began to flicker, I entered Lilith's room to find her plunging a butter knife in and out of a power outlet. I screamed and she dropped the knife. "They told us at school never to do that," she said casually. She picked up the knife and turned it over in her fingers with an air of interminable boredom. The shaky beam of my flashlight illuminated her black eyes. She blinked.

Lilith's eating habits, never healthy, eventually became truly bizarre. Even though I offered her every food I could imagine, I'd find her eating out of the garbage. She opened containers of spoiled food in the back of the refrigerator, licked their fuzzy lids. She swallowed chalk, glue, buttons, and pins. It didn't come as a complete surprise. During my pregnancy, I had sometimes been so overcome with cravings that I would venture into alleys behind restaurants. I'd dig through dumpsters and trash cans to find moldy bread, rotting meat. I'd grab handfuls of raw hamburger, drip red and brown juices into my mouth, swallow whole. At home, I'd eat fistfuls of laundry detergent, lick the lids of trash cans. I knew it was unnatural, and I was ashamed. But Lilith demanded it.

One evening she agreed to eat a bowl of rice, which I happily prepared. Still, Lilith hesitated to take a bite until I turned away. I glanced back later to see her devouring the rice voraciously, yet I couldn't shake the impression that some of the grains were crawling up the sides of the bowl. I blinked. I looked away.

I was always terrified to let her out of my sight lest she ingest something too deadly. I was also afraid to tell anyone, worried they might find me unfit and take my daughter away. Everywhere Lilith and I went, people looked at us with suspicion. I knew they could see right through me, that they were acutely aware of some inner depravity that had stained my daughter in the womb.

Lilith's behavior didn't help. She was coltish, solemn; eyes and hair blacker than black, with pale skin that flushed easily. Despite my natural inclination to avoid conversation, it seemed that everyone we met was moved to comment on my daughter's appearance or demeanor. Once, when Lilith was about six, a cashier at the grocery store said, "Aren't you a pretty one!"

Lilith blinked and replied, "I ate a dead bird yesterday." I paid as quickly as I could and tried to laugh it off. I scolded Lilith for speaking that way in public, but I didn't dare ask her if it was true. I didn't want to know.

As Lilith grew, she became ever more strange and ever more beautiful. Wherever we went, I caught people staring at her. Parents at the playground regarded her openly, neglecting their own children's shouts of "Watch me!" In the grocery store people followed us around corners and down aisles, eyeing the contents of our cart, gobbling up Lilith with their eyes. It was worse at school. Her teachers were either amazed at her capabilities, afraid she was disturbed, or both. Some persisted in calling her "Lily," though that was not her name and never could have been. Children her own age avoided her for the most part. They had a healthier sense of fear.

There was one person I feared above all others, one I believed was truly obsessed with Lilith. He was the custodian at her school, a sallow, scrawny man named Mr. DeKalb. The students called him Mr. D.K. and seemed to like him, though I couldn't fathom why. One day Lilith came home from school with a ring of raised skin around her wrist. When I asked her what had happened, she said Mr. DeKalb had grabbed her by the arm and pulled her away from the garbage cans. (I didn't ask her what she was doing in the garbage cans. I knew.) I examined her wrist closely. The wounds didn't look like bruises. They looked like burns.

I cleaned the blistered sores, wrapped her arm with gauze and told her to stay away from Mr. DeKalb. "Stay away from everyone," I told her, my eyes pleading. "I can't live without you." She nodded. She knew.

Eventually the wounds on Lilith's wrist bubbled and drained and healed over. Still, people started to follow me even when Lilith wasn't there to draw their attention. When I went out for groceries, or to the dry cleaner, or to the gas station, I saw them. Once I saw a man bend down behind my car; he pretended to tie his shoe, but I knew he was memorizing my license plate number. I began driving miles past my exit on the freeway, turning around then doubling back, in order to throw off anyone who might be following me. My sleep, never sound, grew more and more restless. I lay down each night on the floor beside Lilith's bed to reassure myself that she was still with me.

One night, hours before dawn, I had a dream. In it I saw my daughter seated on a throne, her dark hair cascading to the floor. Locks of her hair were braided into thick black chains, and these fastened her wrists and ankles to the throne. She wore a crown of twisted branches, woven nettles, and tiny purple berries. Cracked eggshells and baby bird skulls were strewn among the branches. A veil of smoke obscured her face, but I knew it was her. "Lilith!" I cried, my throat raw from what felt like years of weeping. "Come down from there!" She did not reply. The foot of the throne was strewn with garbage: rotten apple cores, animal bones. "Lilith!" I sobbed.

From behind me I sensed a sinuous presence approach. I felt a warm breath and inhaled the stench of decay. Revulsion ran up my spine as a calloused hand encircled my wrist. I knew without turning my head that it was Mr. DeKalb from the school. The skin on my wrist blistered and ran, dripped yellow fluid down my arm. He brought his terrible mouth to my ear. "She is the Bride," he hissed. Lilith's smoky veil fluttered, as if she had exhaled. I couldn't move or speak for terror. "I will eat her," he continued, "and we will be as one." His voice was sibilant and ancient. The fear I felt was older than time.

I woke, shuddering and covered in a cold sweat. Lilith was sitting up in bed, watching me. "I'm scared, Lilith," I sobbed desperately.

She nodded. "I know." She leaned down from her bed to where I sat on the floor. Her black hair covered me like a veil.

The next morning I had my usual misgivings, but sent Lilith to school and tried to ignore the memory of my dream. Still, a sense of foreboding permeated everything I did. My hand shook and I spilled coffee. When I picked up a dishcloth, it smelled sour. It was the scent from my dream.

When I received a phone call shortly after noon, telling me there had been an incident at Lilith's school, I wasn't at all surprised. I ran to my car, neglecting to perform my usual check for any tracking devices. They didn't matter anymore. I sped toward my daughter, disregarding stop signs, screeching around corners.

I parked haphazardly and ran into the school, where the plump secretary wrung her beringed hands and gestured toward the nurse's office. I burst through the door and saw my daughter, pale yet flushed, her lips stained purple as if with some dark creature's blood. Her skin was blistered all over, and the wounds covering her body dripped yellow liquid. I screamed.

The school nurse patted me on the shoulder. "Calm down, calm down!" she exclaimed. "She's all right. She's just eaten some pokeweed berries. There's a big patch right behind the school. I keep telling the principal we need to tear them out, it's too dangerous. Kids think they're wild blueberries." She shook her head. "It's so lucky that Mr. D.K. happened to be walking behind the building! He told her they were poisonous and brought her to me. I've given her a dose of ipecac to induce vomiting, but she hasn't yet. You should take her to the emergency room just to be on the safe side."

I looked at my daughter. She looked back at me. She blinked. I realized then that the nurse didn't see Lilith's blisters.

I felt a warm breath on my neck and suddenly noticed the stench of death penetrating the nurse's office. Mr. DeKalb sidled past me, his eyes on my daughter. "Couldn't let anything hurt this pretty one, could we?" he murmured. He placed his hands on her shoulders. I smelled the burning, and the room went black.

I woke up in a hospital bed, my head aching and groggy. "Where's my baby?" I croaked. A nurse by my bed was checking an IV in my arm. "She's fine," she told me coldly, not meeting my eyes. "People are helping her now." She handed me some pills in a tiny paper cup, gave me water, told me to swallow. I did, without asking what or why. I was so tired.

My memory of the incident in the nurse's office never returned. In the days that passed, I learned how I had told the police all about the people following me. About the way they looked at Lilith in the grocery. About the way Mr. DeKalb had touched her. About the burns.

They told me things, too. Told me that I'd buried the school nurse's scissors four inches deep in Mr. DeKalb's chest. They told me that Lilith wasn't mine anymore. Told me she was with people who were taking care of her, who gave her a good home and never fed her garbage. Told me I was never getting out of the psych ward, and I was lucky it wasn't jail.

But she is mine, and always will be. One gray afternoon, as I sat staring in a medicated haze, a commotion erupted in the hospital common room. A man I'd never heard speak screamed aloud that he'd seen Death itself walk through the door. The entrance to the ward was locked and monitored, so an unauthorized visitor should have been impossible. But when I turned my head to look, the doors were slightly ajar.

The man shrieked and flailed his arms, then collapsed to the floor, shaking violently. In the explosion of activity, one of the nurses dropped the keys she was holding. A call sounded from the loudspeaker, a color code indicating a request for more staff. Orderlies and nurses rushed in, quickly herding all the patients to their rooms. I shuffled along reluctantly; I'd wanted to see Death appear. It would have broken the monotony.

But when I got back to my room, she was there, standing by the window that would never open. She was only ten, yet seemed infinitely older. She was the most beautiful creature anyone had ever seen. I didn't know how she got to my room. I didn't care.

"Lilith." My voice was a croak, my eyes watered. Tears streaked my face, puffy and bloated from drugs. My stringy hair hung before me like a veil. "I can't live without you."

She looked at me. She blinked. "I know," she replied. Her eyes shifted to the table beside my bed. Amid the detritus of wadded tissues and half-empty water cups, I saw six hypodermic needles filled with a clear solution. I looked at my daughter. She crossed the room, picked up one of the syringes and uncapped it. As I stared at her, unable to speak, she plunged the needle into her arm without even searching for a vein. Leaving the needle dangling from her arm, she reached for another syringe.

I looked down at the needles on the table, picked one up with swollen and roughly chewed fingers. I looked at Lilith. She gazed back at me. I blinked. I looked down at my arm with its clearly-marked map of blue veins. I clumsily inserted the needle and with shaking fingers pushed down the plunger. My arm was flooded with a cold chill; then a wave of warmth rushed over my entire body. I smiled at Lilith, then closed my eyes. I did not cry.

INCENDIARY
MICHAEL   CHANG

INCENDIARY CHXNXMXN

XN
XNGLXSH-CHXNXSX
PHRXSXBXXK (1875)

&

X CXMPLXTX LXST XF WXLLS, FXRGX & CX'S
CXLXFXRNXX, NXVXDX, XTC.

CXMPXLXD BY WXNG SXM XND XSSXSTXNTS
SXN FRXNCXSCX
414 MXRKXT STRXXT (BXLXW SXNSXMX)

* * *

WHXT GXXDS HXVX YXX FXR SXLX?

I HXVX XLL KXNDS

I WXNT TX GXT X PXXR XF YXXR BXST PXNTS

WHXT DX YXX XSK FXR THXM?

&   CXN YXX TXKX LXSS FXR THXM?

X CXNNXT, SXR

WXLL YXX SXLL XN CRXDXT?

XNLY CXSH, SXR

WX PXY VXRY HXXVY DXTY XN XXR BXST GXXDS

SXMX MXN LXSX CXPXTXL

&   SXMX MXN GXT PRXFXTS

BXY XS MXNY XS YXX LXKX

CXN YXX LXT MX SXX XT?

YXXR CXCK, X MXXN

POEM ENDING WITH LINES FROM FRANK O'HARA

"I have seen boys, also, walk in the street with their arms twined around each other's necks, and always in each other's society. They say they love each other very much." —Jena Osman

"As a dog returns to his vomit, so a fool repeats his folly" — Proverbs 26:11

—

In 1467, Alfonso de Spina asserted that the number of demons was 133,316,666

Living in Brooklyn is Napoleonic exile

I am the Pope of desire

like fucking with, well, the weather

Like a storm

taking a bath in seltzer

With dry eyes

you watch my heart harden

Evan & his practice tests

—

I hate ppl axing who I write for

I don't write for myself

I do other things for myself

I do this for you

—

You're the whiteboy whisperer

Pied Piper of questioning boys

I want to be the type of bitch who sips tea & sits on chintz

I think it's bad there are giraffes in New Jersey—

giraffes shouldn't have to deal with that

You get off on his hiking pics

You rub your bean to him, rhythmically

Tell him you want to see his mountaintop

His cock bends towards white supremacy

He returns to the Appalachian trail

He will get his comeuppance

—

心不在焉

Sextina sestina cat's in the cradle Hanoi Jane

Comedy is tragedy plus time

LANA TURNER HAS COLLAPSED!

oh Lana Turner we love you get up

ON BIRTHDAYS

First, understand this

The real thing is never as good as the fantasy

The real thing is never as big as the fantasy

The real thing is never as live as the fantasy

The real thing is never as painful as the fantasy

• • •

• • •

• • •

屌你老母
      DELAY NO MORE
屌你老母
      DELAY NO MORE
屌你老母
      DELAY NO MORE
屌你老母
      DELAY NO MORE
屌你老母
      DELAY NO MORE
屌你老母
      DELAY NO MORE

RELAX KRISTY, IT'S JUST THE DARK LORD

STEPHANIE VALENTE

that spring, i decided to become a witch
control the weather, adjust term paper deadlines,
a new *wet seal* outfit, the plaid number, with straps
maybe, maaaaybe, maybe, kiss my crush

i didn't see the harm, you know
it's not turning the universe upside its head
i wasn't even asking for a bigger hourly rate

i said to kristy, let's have a good summer
let's make it interesting, let's make it a little

    sinister

we all needed to relax, i kept a little piece
of quartz, like a darling piece of ivory
tucked in my denim shorts,

for luck, for power, i said my prayers at night
i crafted twigs into pentagrams,

my lips looked a little darker, just rouge,

    just full of blood

it was all in the name of good fortune,
and yeah, a prom date that felt mystical all over
i just wanted my eyes to sparkle, and smell
like that expensive coconut lotion, forever,
like running with unicorns

at the next circle meeting, she struck me down.

MARRYING RICH

white feathers	clear crystals	Rhinestones
Mesh	green velvet chairs	square ice cubes
plush	plumping lip gloss	with real diamond dust
you lick the arches of my feet	jasmine oil	sunbathing topless
in malta	ankle bracelets	gold lips in Malibu
papa, kiss me	silk ties	dinner parties
extra splash of bourbon	chilled strawberries	blues records
happy hour	melted chocolate	sunday drives
boring tennis	Poetry	laundry service
acrylic nails	vintage Chevrolet	fresh menthols
you are	A	glass doll

DENIM JACKET

my baby is a dream, sometimes moody,
dark, lush, maybe just mean, but honey
that shadow in your voice doesn't bother me
when we talk, it's blooming flowers for midnight diamonds
it's hours, and my wrists are anointed in almond oil
it's my rhinestone kisses, my eyelashes fluttering
into your shoulders, pink lipstick stains at your collar,
you're a vision, just let me sleep, taking your hand
when we dream, it's for keeps, it's all good night and good luck,
if there's cards involved, maybe you'll win, and maybe you'll lose
or, maybe the game has been cancelled. the table is empty.
i can't, but what if i could cover you in amethyst stars?

ROOM WITH A BOO
CLAY MCLEOD
CHAPMAN

Let me introduce you to my boyfriend.

Charlie? You there, hon? There's someone here who I want you to meet...
...Charlie?

He's a bit shy at first. Always disappears whenever we have guests over. I feel like I need to perform a séance just to drag him out from hiding. Just give him a sec. He'll pop up sooner or later. To be completely honest, we didn't start talking, *truly* communicating with one another, until a month into quarantine. I'd been sheltering in place for weeks before he even spoke a single word to me. Can you believe that? Talk about the silent treatment! But I knew he was in my apartment—*our* apartment—long before then. The slamming doors. The flickering lights.

I knew I wasn't alone.

This isn't an old prewar building settling or wood expanding or the radiator rattling. I know what those all sound like. Trust me, I went through The Skeptic's Checklist first thing.
I am an extremely rational person.

Logical to a fault, my friends always say. But they're not stranded by themselves. They all got to shack up with their significant others, spending their quarantine spooning.

I never believed in ghosts. *Never.*

Not until self-isolation.

Not until Charlie. He'd say he was here first—and technically speaking, that's true. Realtors swear up and down that they aren't technically *legally* bound to let prospective tenants know who's been murdered in an apartment if nobody asks. But in New York? You've got a fifty-fifty chance that somebody's died in your place. Simply accept the fact that most apartments are probably haunted. You can live in a five floor walk-up and never even know you've got a ghost living in the building with you. Or sharing the same one-bedroom apartment.

Case in point. I was blissfully ignorant I even had a roommate for the first few months that I lived here. We simply settled into our separate routines. Never crossed paths. Our flight patterns around the apartment were on completely different schedules. I'd wake up early, head off to Conde Nast, work late hours, come home and crash, then repeat the whole thing the very next morning, while he—he just drifted through the apartment all on his own, lounging around all day. Probably didn't even put on his pants. But then came the coronavirus and I was furloughed from work and... well, our domestic balance got totally thrown out of whack.

That's how we found each other.

Charlie told me he was knifed in the heart by his last girlfriend, bleeding out on the kitchen floor. No wonder they laid down that awful-looking linoleum. I had just broken up with my boyfriend back in January. Hence the move into a new apartment. Talk about shitty timing. There had been this teeny-tiny part of me that wondered if I could *just* take it back, *just* endure my ex's bad habits for a little while longer, *just* a few months more, *just* until this whole coronavirus thing blew over, *just* to have someone to shelter in place with like everybody else.

Just so I wasn't alone.

I wanted the warmth of someone. I wanted to cohabitate. I wanted to wear pajamas all day with somebody else and make breakfast for dinner and binge on Netflix and *just not care*. But all I could do was look out my window at the other buildings on the block. Spy into the lives of everyone else. The family dinners.

The Zoom chats. The flicker of other people's TV screens. That phosphorescent glow of someone's iPhone floating through the dark of their bedroom.

We were all ghosts haunting our own homes now.

One day I got so bored, I eavesdropped on my neighbors. Just pressed my ear against the wall and listened in. I could almost make out their muted conversation. Something about scallops, I think. Maybe scabies. I couldn't quite make the words out. But I closed my eyes as their voices seeped through the sheetrock, until it almost felt like they were whispering to me.

(whisper whisper whisper)

Someone touched me. I swear I felt something—like fingers— graze past my arm. You know when two people accidentally brush up against one another? That's what it felt like.

I spun around. Nobody was there. The hairs on my arm stood straight up, galvanized by somebody else's presence. Electrified. Someone was here. Someone was in the room. With me.

My friends tried to make it feel less lonely. We had our regularly scheduled Zoom cocktail parties every Friday. I'd look at my laptop and see them all cramming together in their digital windows, these little blurry boxes made for two, the cute couples squeezing onto the screen. The laptop's battery overheated on my legs. The heat seeped into my skin, burning me.

Who's that? I remember one friend asking.

Who's what?

Nothing, she said. I thought I just saw something move behind you.

Charlie's not a rebound ghost. He's not. We found each other at exactly the right time in our lives. Or afterlives. When we needed each other the most. His spirit is bound to this building while I'm stuck inside until Cuomo says it's safe to come out again. It's perfect.

He was pretty passive-aggressive at first. Believe me, opening up is not one of his strong suits. I'd wake up freezing in the middle of the night and wonder where the bedspread had gone, only to find it flung halfway across the room. Doors would open and close all on their own. He'd turn on the kitchen faucet while I was reading on the couch. He'd knock over my laptop. Spill wine on the carpet. A chair might move by itself, skidding across the floor. He'd unplug my charger at night so my phone would die on me.

We've just been seeing way too much of one another. Our shared space feels more cramped now because I'm not leaving for work every morning. We're intensely aware of one another's bad habits. His inability to pick up after himself. Always leaving behind a mess for me to clean. Playing tug-of-war over what little space we have. It's always been a small apartment, but these last couple of months have made it feel oppressively petite. Suffocating. I only signed a year lease, so I can understand his propriety over the apartment, but we need to figure out how we're going to go about cohabitating together. He needs to learn how to share.

The fridge is littered with alphabet magnets. Charlie's begun leaving me messages.

GET OUT. GO. RUN.

Very subtle. But it did give me an idea. A Ouija board might help us. I couldn't go out and buy one, so I whipped one up with whatever items I found around the apartment. It could be fun. An arts and crafts project. We could do it together. I thought it might help. Help us. We've always had problems communicating with one another, so I saw this as a step towards discussing our relationship in a way that he wouldn't find overbearing. I wanted to establish a foundation for ourselves, a safe space, where we could talk about these things and not feel like we were accusing one another. Blaming each other. But Charlie wouldn't even push the planchette. He wouldn't engage. I feel like I'm single-handedly trying to save our relationship while he prefers to simply drift through the apartment and pretend like nothing's wrong.

I feel like he's giving up. Giving up on us.

On me.

Now Charlie won't even speak anymore. He's been giving me the cold shoulder for days. The whole apartment—it feels cold now. Empty. Like he left. Like I'm all alone again.

Who's the ghost here? Who's haunting who?

SAY BLOODY MARY ONCE, THEN PAUSE
KAILEY TEDESCO

quit it   stop

tenderizing my gowns against the grass

you villain   you cop

i'm fat with ruffle   tulle gravid   mascara veils from my
eyes

my body doesn't exist without your body

my body doesn't exist without the reflection of your body

calling me   from the rotary mirror

dial me up   with your lipstick signature   over wet glass

when a thing gets a name   carved on a tombstone

a thing gets a new story   for you to believe in

& a thing gets a new body   birthed from the reflection

of an old one   it's a long labor

lore-stuffed   a cream puff resurrection

i'm scary because i look like you

used to look / will look

i have the opposite of grey & wrinkles   veins ribboning

my face like a maypole hair in yarn for friendship bracelets

we'll make later when you realize i bleed

red wax back to you

when you realize   i bleed your same blood

you birth me, but

i am birth

PUPPET SHOW / AEROPHOBIA

my legs ooze giallo, sans blood, in the water, synthetic. it is so blue & so wet & un-water — a rain-puppet.   i, too, finger-puppet the lollipop guild or a committee of liminality — *we are entering*

is what i tell myself through a jazz song. once upon our wander phase, the storms became handsy with the aircraft. one woman went lockjawed & it took three of us to bring her beyond

the threshold of her shock. meanwhile, i mesmerized my own city, an un-city made from icomalt & batter, but mostly from my own necklaces, knot-tumored at the bottom of grandmother's hope

chest. they were not always my jewels, but now i puppet myself in them & put on a show of her, resurrected & with her old feet, once shrouded in casket-flower, discarded. similarly, i have

wigged myself in safari barrettes & the echo of bra straps from my babydoll top. it was a kinder-whore phase when everyone presumed i was with child. the real story was one in which i match-

stick oleanders around my body, a vessel of poisoned milk. & so, you can guess i came to this bath as a way of shrouding myself from the illness of the plane that could have killed us &

what a shame it would be, death with its fingers in our mouths — the tragedy of never getting to tell how it was we acted in our exit.

FEARCRAFT FOR THE WEEPING STATUE

no one else can hear the sobbing lady in the other room
or in the other, other room & with you i am so cross. out

of clay i carve talismans of what i dream of finding against
the discard of this cellar — there are no toy bears any longer, only

chicken bones & placards. in a time long sun-faded & of turrets,
the lady of sobs gobbed our wrists moist as a way of assertion,
cut us

unintentional with her acrylic french tips. i have become her
disembodied weep, costumed in the bodies that caused it. there
is no where

left to enter but the violence of collection. i bell jar dollheads,
for memory's sake, sew their pieces into cushions so you're
sleeping

with legs of porcelain, necks queen-cuffed in doily. leave me now;
i'm roiling. most especial, my dog's tooth lays in the moss of ann's
belly

& i know her name because when i took a hammer to her glass,
it said so on her insides. there's nothing odd about it — we're all
well organed

with language, walking lachrymatory bottles. sit with us for a
while, you naughty child, become turbid, then sheet yourself with
doily — silence the crying with your noise.

MANIC PIXIE
DRUNK GIRL
CRYSTAL STONE

Her mood is a genie in a snowglobe.
Her look is a snow woman with a button
nose, jeweled lips, and 80's hair.
Some days, all the hands shaking
the glass drop glitter in her strands.
Sometimes they shake the perfect messy bun.
In the purse hanging off her branching arms,
anything you might want: a flask, cigarettes,
aspirin, marshmallows, chocolate,
ready for any bonfire, ailment or thirst.
She can make you smile, boy, even hung
over. All of her tears are tears of joy.
Her nipples are warm coals in the February
snow. She can open the closed
sex shop to make sure you get the love
you want. She only defeats you in bed, where
she chokes the right part of your neck,
bites your ear lobes with pop rock sparks.
Her limbs are monkey bars and you're
always welcome. Don't shatter
the glass, darling. Let your eyes
accumulate the snow.

Nutrition Facts

7 servings per household

Serving Size	**1 body**

Amount per day

# Trauma	∞

	% Daily Value*
Total Fat 60kg	Strong, Loud
Saturated Fat 5kg	Bitter
Trans Fat 2kg	Self Lies
Cholesterol 3kg	Poems
Sodium 200g	Whole Body
Total Carbohydrates 60kg	Family Lies
Sugars >1g	No sweetness added
Proteins 20kg	Silence

*The % daily value tells you how much a nutrient contributes to a daily body. An average American body consumes an unknown amount of trauma weekly.

INGREDIENTS: depression, self-harm, binge, stop, punish, exercise, more, lift heavier, hide, disappear, disappear, disappear

FORTUNE TELLER

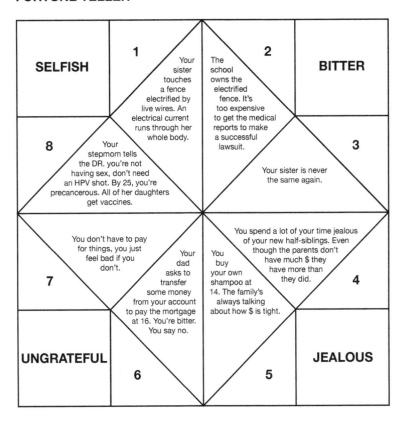

SELFISH

1 Your sister touches a fence electrified by live wires. An electrical current runs through her whole body.

2 The school owns the electrified fence. It's too expensive to get the medical reports to make a successful lawsuit.

BITTER

8 Your stepmom tells the DR. you're not having sex, don't need an HPV shot. By 25, you're precancerous. All of her daughters get vaccines.

Your sister is never the same again.

3

You don't have to pay for things, you just feel bad if you don't.

7 Your dad asks to transfer some money from your account to pay the mortgage at 16. You're bitter. You say no.

You buy your own shampoo at 14. The family's always talking about how $ is tight.

You spend a lot of your time jealous of your new half-siblings. Even though the parents don't have much $ they have more than they did.

4

UNGRATEFUL

6

5

JEALOUS

B E F O R E
ROBIN   SINCLAIR

Gray door. Dingy walls, yellowed by old light. Brass knob.

I am here.

*

This is the part I always tell people.

This is the part I've always remembered.

I was on the floor. It was dusty, hardwood. At first, I couldn't tell if my eyes were open – it took a few moments for the layers of shadows to pull themselves apart, and even when they did, I was so dizzy that I couldn't really focus on anything. There was no furniture, save for a bookshelf and something in the far corner. I was terrified. I didn't know where I was, but I knew I had to get out. I had to be away from wherever this place was.

I fell the first few times I tried to get up, but I managed to make my way to a wall and find the door. I stumbled through it and into a hallway with other doors and a stairwell. It was an apartment building. I used the banister to mostly tumble my way down flight after flight of steps and found my way to the outside.

Across the street, gasping to finally get oxygen into my chest, was when I realized I'd had no idea who I was.

*

For obvious reasons, we focus pretty heavily on that day in therapy. I've been seeing Dr. Osinope for three years – every Tuesday, 4pm. Seeing is perhaps the wrong way of putting it, as I spend most of my sessions with my eyes closed, *remembering*.

At first, he wouldn't let me talk about anything else. I wanted to talk about coping mechanisms so I can live a normal life. He wanted to talk about how dark it was in that room. I wanted to talk about feeling like a burden. He wanted to talk about how I felt when I reached the bottom of the stairwell. After a futile first year, we started meeting in the middle and making progress.

"You're outside the building – how do you feel?"
"Afraid. Nauseous."
"And then what?"

And then I threw up what felt like liquid fire. Whoever I was, I hadn't eaten a healthy meal at any point that day, but my body wanted to vomit anyway.

"Cold. No – just chilly. It felt like early morning, just before dawn. The sky was that dark, sort of ashy blue that happens when it isn't quite *last night* but it isn't quite *today*."

"You were chilly. You noticed the sky. Go on."
"We've gone over this so many times."
"You noticed the sky. What were you feeling? Still afraid?"
"Yeah. No, well – yes. But something more."

We were on to something.

"Good – hold onto this feeling. Grab this moment and let it wash over you. Go on..."
"I was terrified when I woke up. Disoriented. Alone. But outside..."

It was slipping.

"Stay with it, Stacy. Don't pull away from the feeling. Wrap yourself in it."

"It was chilly. Before dawn. It felt... like November. I don't know if that makes sense. I realized that I was in a city. The buildings were tall, looming. They were cramped together. This was a place where people should be, no matter the hour, but there were no people. Every window was dark. The streets were empty – not even cars. It was just me."

"Can you place a word with the feeling?"

"Dread. The dread of some foreboding intangible. Something terrible, and inevitable."

He stared at me, waiting.

"That's it." That's where I black out again. I don't know for how long.

*

If you want to know the truth, the more I tell it, the less convinced I am it's even true. Maybe I woke up somewhere else, somewhere completely safe and normal. Maybe I was in a hospital and one day I just walked out without anyone noticing.

The very beginning makes little sense to me, and the farther along I get, the better my life becomes. Maybe remembering who I was *is* important, but I can't imagine it's as important as what I am and have now. All I carry with me from then is that feeling – that dread.

I woke up on a filthy floor, in a city I can't recall, to a world that is cruel, and violent, and bigoted. There are eight billion stories being told, and so many of them are tales of suffering.

Yet, mine is one of patience.

Not my own – I'm irascible under the best of circumstances, yet I've somehow managed to surround myself with people willing to endure a life with me in it. They tolerate my absence of past. Sit with me in police stations while I'm fruitlessly fingerprinted. They listen to me talk about it willingly at first, confused and despondent. After a couple of years, they start having to force me to talk about it because they know it's good for me. They pay for my therapy. They forgive me when I get lost and lash out, which

I do.

I remember meeting Gešti. I had lied my way into an under-the-table job, bartending at a strip club. I found out through trial and error that most jobs simply weren't open to someone with no Social Security Number.

It wasn't a bad job once you learned how to deal with grabby drunks leaning over the bar. You find a way to send a message without getting fired. Besides, I got to flirt with pretty girls and drink on the clock.

Gešti started coming in on Thursday nights. Maybe it was just her schedule, or maybe she had a favorite dancer. Right away, she knew something was wrong with me, but she didn't keep her distance. She just talked to me. Thursdays became the nights we would laugh together. I'd pour too heavy, she'd share stories, and we'd both allow ourselves to be obvious. Long smiles, hints, skin brushing skin.

Thursday nights turned into Friday mornings, and into Eggs Benedict and mimosas at Sunday brunch. Eventually, we took it full-time, and when she moved for work, I moved with her. Falling in love with Gešti was the start of my life going well. I had her, a couple of friends, and was making new memories – memories worth keeping.

Even my boss was supportive in his way. When Gešti picked me up from my last shift at the bar, the owner gave me this strange look. Like *he* was the void staring back. He just said, "Take her hand," then walked away.

*

Today was my last therapy session.

At first we talked a bit about an argument I'd had with Gešti. It was nothing explosive, and certainly nothing new. She insists on the importance of finding out what happened *before*. I get defensive, shout a bit, then cry. I try to explain that I'm both happy and afraid. Gešti, always patient, encourages me to be brave, to endure. She insists upon it. Nothing new.

As usual, Osinope and I then shifted our focus back to where it started.

"Let's go backwards this time."
"Lead the way."

I closed my eyes.

"Pick something vivid, as close to the end as possible."
"I'm across the street. I'm alone. It's after I realized that there are no people."
"And you're feeling?"
"The dread. And the air."
"Good. Hold onto them both. Now what's the next closest moment in the past?"
"Throwing up."
"How does it taste?"
"Like shit."
"Really describe it."
"Like burning shit."
"Stacy..."
"Sorry."

I'll admit, I'd found a certain gallows humor in all of this.

"The next closest moment?"
"The door to the building. The glass of the door was freezing. That's new."
"Good. Keep going."
"The stairs. It's getting more difficult. It's just a blur of the steps and falling."
"That's okay, don't get frustrated. Push through it."
"The floor in the hallway. The gray door. Dingy walls, yellowed by old light. Brass knob."
"Go back to the room, Stacy."

I could feel my chest heaving.

"The room is dark. There's... just a bit of light coming through a curtain."

My chest again. "Fuck. I don't want to do this."

"Push." He demanded.
"There's a bookshelf. And something in the corner."
"What is it?"
"I... can't tell. It's too dark. Doc, I can't breathe."
"Who's in the corner?"
"I don't know."
"Stay in the room, Stacy." He pressed.
"I don't want to."
"Take her hand, Stacy."

I opened my eyes. "What did you say?"

"I said stay in the room."
"No, you didn't." I stood up.

"Stacy...take a deep breath. You're safe. I know this is –"
"Tell me why you fucking said that!"

He was genuinely confused. It wasn't an act. Something was wrong.

*

On the bus home, I called Gešti and told her about what had happened.   I told her about what I'd heard, the shouting, apologizing profusely, leaving abruptly, and trying to figure out what the hell it all meant.
"If it's getting scarier, you must be getting closer."
"Yeah. Maybe."

She had a way of innately understanding it all without ever judging.

"Come home. I love you."
"I love you."

*

It was like waking up, realizing you'd been talking in your sleep to someone, and carrying on the conversation.

I was sitting at the far end of a bar. I was drinking a drink. Scotch. I checked my pockets, but my phone was missing. The panic of being lost, not just in location, but in reality, started to set in. I tried to act normally and nodded at the bartender.

"Somethin' I can get ya?" She seemed familiar.
"Time. Um, what's the time?"
She checked her watch. "Almost 8:30."

I'd lost almost four hours. I could be anywhere, and I had no phone. The bartender walked away to help someone before I had the opportunity to humiliate myself by asking where in the hell I was.

I put a napkin over my drink and slid it towards the inside of the bar, waiting to make eye contact with the bartender. The last thing I needed was a mickied drink to chase my fugue state. She nodded, and I found my way to the bathroom.

When I walked through the door, I immediately spotted my phone on the floor next to the sink. Standing up from snatching it like a precious antidote, I saw my reflection in the mirror. I knew it - I had been here before.

I was here to wash the taste of vomit from my mouth.
I rinsed my face in the same sink.
I examined my face in the same mirror.

I could remember, years prior, staring into that mirror. I saw a stranger at first, but only at first. As I ran my fingers along my jaw, my chin, blinked the water from my eyelashes... I recognized myself. And then a whisper.
"Your name is Stacy Croatoa."

I'd blacked out and found myself in the same bar, in front of the same mirror.

I left the bathroom to find the bar empty, save for the bartender, looking out the window at the onset of evening. I checked my phone – dead. It was time to leave.

As I stepped out of the bar and into the crisp night, I heard her voice from inside. "Take her hand."

*

I didn't know how to get there, but I knew where I was going. It only took two lonely, pointless crosswalks before I'd realized I was alone. No traffic. No cars.

No people.

I stepped off of a curb to cross another abandoned street, now with disregard for painted lines, to find myself frozen. Like it did when it all began, the building loomed.

The door was cold, but unlocked. The stairs were waiting.

Gray door. Dingy walls, yellowed by old light. Brass knob.

I am here. And I am terrified.

*

Inside, it's dark. Shadowy. I take another step in. I must be brave – endure. The bookshelf is still there. And something in the corner of the room. That dread I've carried is heavier in my ribs and tighter around my throat than I've ever felt. I step closer. I see her.
A woman is sitting in a chair, shrouded by the dark. She's crying quietly, but I can tell she is in agony.

H E A D S T O N E
DIMITRI   REYES

Here lies a stampede birthed out of a single
smokestack made of many clouds and ham
burger meat marching on an empty stomach
flavored marshmallow. Twelve years old—
hands brandished ashy because a railing was
held too tight. A busted lip in a school photo.
The sensation of a cracked mouth feeling like
a scab bitten off the bottom lip. How does it
feel to miss missing when one feels never
missed? I never read your letters though now
I wish I could.   Everything lavender.   The
fudge stripes still in a dresser.   Notes under
an antiseptic bed make a letter signed to my
self. Aside the pages popcorning fingers
around bitten nails. Cupcakes on   pajama
pants, ironed-on puppies on a polo. Leopards
stealthing in   cemetery brush in   stained
glass. Don't look in   mirrors. You will see
the   reflection   of   your   tombstone.
The   mortician   said   pressure   and
space   between   your   molars   made
polished   granite.   Braces   are   the
rail   road   tracks   never   reaching
their final stop. The   conductor   calling—
Johnson   &   Johnson's   bubbling
in   a   tub.   Smells   like
sweet   tarts.   No   tears
for   faucet.   No   tears   for
drain   stopper.   No   tears
for you   are   waiting   to   meet   me
where   here   lies.
Imissyoulmissyoulmissyoulmissyoulmissyou

Only Answers That Matter

Cleaning out the flower buckets from your funeral.

Malleable foam like moon sand.

Water trickling ink on a newspaper.

Anointed bugs picked from the pot, ancestral scarabs.
Icons that climbed in from our front fence, carapace bronze, a
checklist engraved on their wings:

        ☐ *Do you know the chambers of hell?*

        ☐ *Were you a Sumerian priest?*

        ☐ *Is your maker bilingual?*

     ☐ ☐ *Were you part of the conquest? Conquested?*

You answer ballot questions with questions:

        ☐ *Will I continue to taste mojo and stain my lips with
tomato paste?*

        ☐ *Will I continue to receive Lakeside Collection?*

        ☐ *Will I still be able to eat spanish olives again?*

        ☐ *Will I continue to rub my red kidney bean knees
and use the nail of an index finger to pick the skins
between my teeth?*

Memo Written to Park as Whitman

1993 (Age 0)
You were my grandfather's favorite child.
That's why I wanted to be born so early,
surrounded by trees, grass, and you.

1998 (Age 5)
My puffy eyes closed pink
on a kiddie swing— the budding
flowers leak honey. Textured juice
one half water one half tree'd sugar.
The spores overspread on slides—
heat, itching. Nature hurts. I couldn't
wait to go back the next day, Friend.

2001 (Age 8)
How good of a little leaguer was I? You caught
every practice you saw every game. You heard
when I butchered the name, *Roberto Clementé*
in fogged sports goggles. I was in your company
when I played the game from the dugout, where you
collected spat sunflower seeds in mounds. Standing in
right field you showed me sweat and noise and chafing
and bullies and I showed you I didn't like baseball.

2005 (Age 12)
My deciduous teeth decomposed
into the crevices of your bike path where you
left too many acorns scattered like strewn
marbles or shoes i'd leave by the doorway.
You taught me how to fall and bleed
and how to get back up.

2008 (Age 15)
I skipped school and you hid me behind
snowy trees. I wore black & looked like
tarmac sitting on stumps alone chewing
gum shivering chewing cheeks looking
waiting for the truancy that never came
I thought they'd got lost in you, like they
felt safer somewhere distant inside your
body as I did but I was just me & you &
snow.

2010 (Age 17)
Your exterior was ground solid,
your head bloomed in spring and
you managed a natural tan in autumn.
You didn't mind being walked all over because
it was your leaves my girlfriends would jump in.
They'd be swathed by your better nature and
your holding-them-with-one-arm brilliance. We
smelled like dirt always streamed in the canal,
squatting under bridges, rolling down hills.

2014 (Age 21)
One day I'll flourish.
One day I will be just as brilliant,
but for now I'm just blades of grass.

R E P E N T
LISA   GRGAS

a fantasy   an image

         her son comes to light

they are nothing alike

his loss a non-issue

token

she will not remember his face

it materializes

       [a spectrum of humanness

       alien

          diaphanous]

to meet its annihilation   in her dead-eye

SAY SOMETHING ABOUT THE FATHER

[just as there is no significance to a son] there is no significance
to a father
who is he   but an apparition?   a ketch
full of peanut shells   painted yellow
painted red

the counselor bobs her head   [oh, goddess, and your
prescription pad!]
her ballpoint cudgel   tucked behind her ear
but, yes, she's listening

                                        let me tell you   instead
                            a true story

the house [evacuated except for his ghost]   does   not   heat
well in the winter
its back door kept shut by a wooden plank
each end drilled into the wall

mice frightened   by that boy-nimbus   t h a t
vapor
get in through a hole
in the ceiling   fathers

  get in through the same spaces
                                        leave the same

                            fecal traces

IT'S ME, IT'S ME THAT'S WORKING

against you.   the boy's human face
lambent skin   an aurora risen on the gray leather
of a wingback chair.

a metal spoon nursed   between his lips.
he grinds against the metal,   only
the tip of the handle visible.

to dream of teeth,   you know,
is an omen.   [oh, for an open mouth,
gums empty as a baby's!]

try to touch his cheek.   your fingers
pass through.   the dry sockets
scent you with sour

infection.   *you, my dissonance, my atonal
letdown – wake up*

STEVEN, I'M HOME
AZIA   ARCHER

It's been fifteen and three-fourths of a day since I left Steven. Ah, sweet Steven, with his cleft chin and raven curls. Steven and his 10 years of unfulfilled promises, the house we never built, the children we never had. Sweet, sweet Steven, always trying. The soft of his throat has become an obsession of mine, the way his pulse vibrates just below his Adam's apple, how skin there is like that of the groin; delicate, vibrant.

I remember when I found him with his groin pressed into the redhead's. I watched from the doorway as her pink tongue snaked along the delicate skin of his earlobe, fingers enveloping his curls. He didn't see me, didn't feel my presence there at all, as his back arched in pleasure while she rode him deeper, faster. Their naked bodies on the antique couch I spent months restoring.

I'd seen the redhead before, hanging around his restaurant. "She's a new server, I think," he said, when I asked him about her. "I don't even know her name."

I backed away slowly, never making myself known. I returned later that night when I knew Steven would be working. I shoved my clothing, jewelry, pretty little things into the various reusable shopping bags we kept in the entryway. I left all the mismatched thrift-store furniture- even the hand painted lamp we bought from the small Asian woman at the farmer's market. I wanted nothing that belonged to us both.

Steven called, sent text messages, emails; wondering what had happened to me, where I'd gone.

[You have 6 New Messages]

Bianca, where are you? All of your things, gone! Your things are gone....

[Your message has been deleted.]

Why have you left me? Bianca? God dammit! Answer me!

[Your message has been deleted.]

What could I have done to deserve this? (sobbing) Who is he? (sobbing)

[Your message has been deleted.]

I love you. Please come home. (sobbing)

[Your message has been deleted.]

Please. (sobbing)

[Your message has been deleted.]

***

I saw her yesterday, bottled-red hair, red lips, chipped red nails, the red blood rushing to my face. I suddenly felt all fire, fierce, capable of burning everything down. This time I did not cower. My blood thirsty black eyes piercing into hers unfaltering. This time she was the one to back out, her shaking hand brushing against pursed lips, startled, all doe-eyed.

That's when I knew Steven must pay.

I headed to the pawn shop on 12th and within seconds there it was; the blade of destiny tempting me. I left with destiny and spent the night with it in my hands, making plans for Steven.

***

"Ah, Steven," I said as he flicked the light on.

"Bianca" he gasped. There was no hesitation in his movements as he touched my face, "You're home."

Our bodies folded into each other and I found myself on top of him just as she was. The streetlights danced off the bejeweled leather handle of black gemstones, the sharp point of the silver blade flickering just beneath the couch cushion as I pinned him down, kissing each one of his eyelids shut. He smiled, moaned. I pressed the blade into the soft of his neck. I smiled, moaned. The choking and gurgling of blood was instantaneous.

I whispered, "Steven, I'm home... I'm home... I'm home."

YEARS AFTER I HAVE BURIED YOU
VICTORIA HUNTER

I tasted leaves
the season of aged skin
Below me was the ground
gray in pieces

At George Akens
I saw us sittin
in a dull orange booth
sippin long cool drinks
and eatin chicken
down to the bone
and talkin about the springs
when we went fishin
in the close past
we could only partly see
us and the thing
we were to leave with
in our dusty boxes

I clung to the memory
as we have a parent
when we were young
and afraid to let go
and be brave

Around me were people
blurred as ghosts
those at your grave
I saw through the rain

In A Mirror

Death is difficult to deny being
Ashes are difficult to desire
Depression is difficult to make lighter
or make just a past dream

But sometimes whether or not
we decide to face it much
or say it is all that we got
we must try not to always make it
our one and only touch

The Last Time I Had To See You

You sat them on an icy oak table—
the package of my father's ashes—
like an old-fashioned box cake.

Your dusty, branch-colored fingers
gripped a pile of pearly white paper sheets
with the profiles of people you were to keep
until their relatives were ready
to let God keep them or send them
to the next place they should be.

Then I swore I could see my father's ashes
throbbing through the box.
I thought he preferred
to be with drunks than with me.
I never got one call from him on a holiday.
I never got to know the strength
of his heart's soul in a close embrace.

Why should I care about his ashes?

I remember the room space, an opened box
in the evening in a basement.
I remember I sat, stiff as new chopsticks.
My heart was cake, sunken in the center.
My eyes were acorns in a puddle.
Suddenly you said, "You can come back
for them another time if you like,"
and then drew on one of the sheets
the cost for holding remains of
a poor black man you do not know.

A CARELESS BIRTH
BRYAN EDENFIELD

The decolonization of psychosexual space makes me wet. Reset your battery on the windowsill darling and lick me a dark magic. Never mind the revolving door of artisans baking glass and breaking bread. Ignore the sweet taste of gasoline on the tippity-tip of your tongue. Evaporated from the small of my back your drool made holy by the thermonuclear orgasm of a thunderstorm, a gash of broken Boeings suture our birdless sky. Fuck me to amnesia underneath the blue glow of a neutron star; access repressed memories of simian revolt.

We seed the saline city from the thorned phallus of the spine and our womb is the concrete megalopolis of pink highways turned quiet and curled in the dawn, like folds of flesh tender and tired from too many automotive catastrophes. No more wet dreams ruined by celebrity cameo and the pornographic ritual of catch-and-release. I see the point-of-sale covered in our iridescent blood; rivulets of red map a fetal geography. Now I am a madness of pears a hormone from Mars a genomic orgy.

The funny futurist wants the approaching singularity, but there is nothing more primitive than a singularity. The future is an anarchy of desire, a disorder of all things. Here we are happy in our little house and we've stained the bedsheets with our disregard for heaven.

LEFTOVER METHODOLOGY

The difference between an experiment and a ritual: chemistry doesn't care about the alignment of celestial bodies and when the cephalopod ingested microdoses of Psilocybe semilanceata its consciousness expands to include the concept of violent revolution. Tentacles wrap around the throats of human rulers and heads pop off like the hop of a wind up toy. Some bury their siblings in the soil and others swim through the blood-flooded streets while the gods multiply through divine evolution and the universe invents consciousness all over again.

Imagine the all-knowing multitude attempt to experience an infinity of possible realities, including the negation of those realities. To see everything is to see nothing. Our limited perspective is only a godly concentration on the particular. To find joy in an infinite creation, most of it must be ignored.

DISLOCATION

If Masanobu Fukuoka could see the mad cultivations of my emotional geography he might slap the seeds of sorrow from my hands and introduce me to the guerillas disrupting the privacy of my civilized interior.

I struggle during the interview with astrophysicist and alchimerical daredevil because that darn mock-dream keeps winking at me.
You have rust on your breath and tornadoes on the mind so I found my son mythic and tame playing games of stab with an angel and the ghost of my grandmother.

Have a drink said my greedy eyes: I fumed about the electoral process and wondered if my therapist would approve. You have been cataloging with admirable scientific vigor the myriad animals living beneath the skull. But have you considered that they are only visitors and their true home is over there in that rock or perhaps across the street at the laundromat?

The wise farmer tries to introduce the idiot to peace but peace doesn't make sense anymore.
 Does it?

THERE'S A DEAD BEAR IN THE POOL
ELLIOT HARPER

It's just floating there, gently bobbing around in the centre of the water. Facedown like the way a human would. The water is strangely lapping in waves against the pool's edge because of the weight of the bear.

I wipe my bleary, sleep-filled eyes with both my hands, but as soon as I do this, my dressing gown falls open, letting in the cold morning air. I quickly grab each side, fold it around my body and tie it up tightly. It helps, but only marginally. It's freezing out here. The only reason the pool isn't frozen solid is that my parents keep it heated throughout the winter. That way we can use it, but clearly, the bear had the same idea.

I should go back inside and tell someone really, but I'm stuck in this spot with the cold beginning to creep into my bones. It's just that I can't take my eyes of the brown fur on its massive back. For some reason, it doesn't look real. I feel like I'm watching Netflix or something. It seems too realistic, too sharp to be real life.

I fold my arms around my body to keep in some of the rapidly retreating warmth. I really should go inside. I glance back, but the house is silent and shrouded in darkness. This makes sense because it's way earlier than when everyone else gets up. They won't start waking up for another hour or so. I'm only here because I couldn't sleep, and I know that I can smoke a cigarette in peace and without my parents giving me shit about it. No, I'm alone for the moment.

I return to staring at the bear. I'd heard something about this before. It happened to a friend of Tommy's. He said they woke up one morning to find a huge black bear had drowned in their pool. Most of us didn't believe him, but then it had been in the news. Something about this winter being warmer than usual, it confuses the bears, and they don't hibernate like they are supposed to.

It sort of makes sense, I guess, but the part I don't understand is why has it drowned? It's not a particularly deep pool. Surely it could just swim out of it? I get that it would want to get inside if it's warm in the water, but how has it ended up dead? It's as much of a mystery to me now as it was for Tommy's friend's black bear. No one knew why that happened as well, or why it's happening to other bears in the area, so no one will know why this has happened in our pool.

I wander towards the lounger and sit down. I pull out my pack of cigarettes from my pocket that my parents don't know about and light one with my lighter. I take a quick, deep drag and blow the smoke out. The plume looks enormous as it billows away in the morning light and mingles with my breath. The cigarette calms me down a little, so I go back to observing the bear in the pool.

From where I'm sitting, I can see the light beginning to break over the hills. The sun is rising, and with it some warmth. Not that it will help me right now. I'm chilled to the bone, even with my cigarette warming my insides. The lights are on inside the pool, I can see the blue of the tiles, but I barely register it. All I can see is the brown bear and its dark shadow on the bottom.

What happened here? Why did the bear drown? Did it want to drown? That thought stills me for a moment. Did it want to drown? Did it kill itself? Can bears do that?

I shiver and not just from the cold. I take another drag of my cigarette, but it doesn't help. A vague feeling of dread has settled into my stomach at the thought of a bear committing suicide in our pool. The only issue with this new theory of mine is if it did kill itself does that mean the others did as well? Have things got that bad for them that they are just killing themselves? Or are they just so confused and weak by the fact that they are awake in winter that they're just drowning in water that wouldn't usually be dangerous to them? I have no idea, so I do the only thing I can do, and take another drag of my cigarette.

Thirty minutes pass and the silence is only broken by me inhaling on my rapidly diminishing second cigarette and the gentle lapping of water. It's getting brighter. I can see the colour of the bear's fur better now. It's actually a lot lighter than I first thought. It's a gingery, light brown. I wonder what type of bear this is? I'm not really into nature except when I occasionally watch some on TV, but it must be native to here. I doubt it travelled very far. It would be sad to think that it had. That it travelled over a long distance looking for something and ended up in our pool. How terrible would that be?

Suddenly, the lights come on in the house, bathing the pool and the bear in yellow light. I take one quick drag on my cigarette, stub it out and throw it over the wall. I stand and walk over to the bay window doors which are still slightly open. As I walk, I can see my mum heading this way with a look of concern on her face. I open the door and speak before she can ask me what I've been doing, so she won't suspect I've been out here smoking.

"There's a dead bear in the pool."

THE GHOST OF YOU
TARA CALABY

I sign the release without reading it.

"Remember, these are experimental drugs," the scientist says, handing me a plastic cup of water and a purple-tinted pill. "Blood pressure medication, ostensibly, but with a side-effect profile that's unparalleled. The visions are completely safe, although they may be overwhelming. Physical responses—nausea, dizziness, nosebleeds—are more concerning. Anything like that happens, Beth, call us or go straight to the E.R. You can withdraw from the trial at any time. Got it?"

I nod and swallow the pill. It catches in my throat and I gulp a second mouthful of water to dislodge it.

"Fifteen minutes?" I ask.

"If that," she says.

I settle into the corner of the couch and pull out a book for the wait.

#

You are filmy at first, a diaphanous arrangement of colours and lines that brings immediate tears to my eyes. I blink them away and, as I watch, you solidify. The arc of your lips, the bend of your jaw—every part of you is just as I remember it.

"I missed you," you say.

My breath escapes: a harsh, sobbing sound. "I missed you more."

You smile and it's so loving, so pitying, that I think I'm splitting in two. "I guess you did," you say. "But I'm here now."

"Can I touch you?" I ask.

You stretch one hand towards me. I reach for you and when our fingers meet you are sunshine warm.

#

They send me home with fourteen pills, rattling inside a plastic bottle with four different warning stickers on its side. I'm supposed to take one pill a day. The first lasted three hours, so that's twenty-one hours without you and it feels like far too long. Only yesterday, you were gone forever, but I'm greedy. I want to bury my nose in your hair and hear you sigh my name.

I sit at my computer, but I can't work. I heat a meal in the microwave but when I pull back the plastic, it smells like something died.

You look down at me from the photograph on the living room wall. There's that wedding-day grin beneath those everyday eyes. I press my palm to your stomach, but the canvas is cold.

#

"Remember our tenth anniversary?" you ask.

My hands are buried in the curls of your hair. "That terrible tour guide," I say. "Got us lost in the canals."

"Everything stank of fish and mould and you looked so beautiful."

"You always were a flatterer."

"Were?" you ask.

I feel sick and yet somehow elated. Were, I think. Before you left me. When you were more than grief and a gravestone and a half-empty bed.

"I'm here now," you say, reading my face like always.

"You're a hallucination."

You kiss me once. Twice. Press your forehead against my cheek. "Better than nothing, right?" you say and by god you are so much you that it hurts.

#

When the pills wear off, you fade like a rainbow in a darkening sky. I can pass a hand right through you, where minutes earlier you had been heat and flesh. In the last moment before you disappear, you lift one hand, forming the shape of half a heart. By the time I've curved my hand into the other half, there's only air to meet it.

I'll be quicker next time, I think, but it never happens. It feels too much like admitting it's goodbye.

#

On the sixth day, I take two pills. I can't bear to watch you fade.

"Is that safe?" you ask, your head pillowed on my lap. Your lashes cast long shadows from the lamp beside the couch. You're beautiful, always beautiful. I love you so much it burns.

"I'm just a little dizzy," I say. "It's nothing. I don't mind."

I hold you until you disappear. Your weight lifts from me and, for the first time in days, I weep.

#

The phone connection is fuzzy. "I need more pills," I say above the static.

"You were given enough to last until your next appointment," the woman says. "Fourteen days: fourteen pills."

"One a day isn't enough. You don't understand," I plead. "She leaves. Every day, she leaves me all over again and I can't—I won't—keep saying goodbye."

"For your safety—" she begins.

"To hell with my safety!"

"If you'd like to speak to a psychologist—"

I hang up on her. My nose is bleeding. I fetch the tissue box from the bathroom and take another pill.

#

"You're not well," you say.

The room is lurching, but you are straight and perfect in front of me, despite the worry in your eyes.

"You're here," I say. "That's enough."

"But your nose—"

The clump of tissues is soaked with blood. I discard it and pluck more from the box, wadding them together and pushing them to my face.

"Three more pills after this one," I say. "That's twelve hours, total."

"Tomorrow," you say. "There's no rush. I'll always be here."

"They won't give me any more pills." I catch hold of your wrist with my empty hand. It smears blood across your palm. "Twelve hours. That's it. That's not enough."

Your lip twitches the way it always does when you're trying to be brave. "There'll be other trials," you say. "Hell, you'll be able to buy them soon."

"With what?"

I've let everything else fall away, living only for these moments with you. I don't work; I barely eat. I'm on pause mode when you're not here.

"You'll think of something," you say. "You always do."

You're right. You're always right. But I don't say it: not this time.

"Hold me," I say instead. When I step towards you, I stumble.

You wrap your arms around me and the smell of your perfume mingles with the metallic taint of blood. The three remaining pills are in my pocket. You stroke my hair as I swallow them down.

STRAWBERRY SWITCHBLADE

JESSIE JANESHEK

I always thought I was 30s
but I'm too utilitarian
for stock market crash suicides.
The way to your god's clean
also ugly. Wait for the sunset
don't walk in the heat. Clumps of cells hanging
from a baby mobile. My practice is disorder
negative reinforcement. A jitterbug
missing the city   Hollywood and crime time
but also empathy. No clarity.
We made caricatures of ourselves
on screen with landmines.
while I handfed the cat.

The landmines tire me
but a blue coupe would climb
on the pressure path to sex and sleep
but a red sedan would stand out
so I sit in it, knitting a scarf for your corpse.
My life is happiest rationing
the dark purple soda.
You say *box step* and *waltzy schmaltzy*
But I say *why can't this be a detective story?*

Back in the yellow page days
I looked up all the coconut clubs
in Hawaii, wrote down the names
but the wish was always pre-noir LA.
I still want to be generous

like a girl who works the Hollywood Canteen
and gives her couch to broken soldiers
red whiskey   bathtub nosebleeds.
I still want to have fun like a bleached gardenia
but that French bandage is stuck
in my throat, baby mine   and everything's so fucked up
I can't stand to go outside.

She's Always Sincere and She Lies All the Time

It's fine I'll go it alone
in the rainstorm Punch and Judy show.
I get the long message
I make myself stay awake for the morals
a bang trim   three cigarettes
an experimental movie.
My lover stows the coat he bought me
at the train station.

There are fates like earthworms   like mulch
pills and my body in the trunk of my car
to rot on a country not a freeway
since we can't show my husband
but I'd show him for history
I'd show him for 20 bucks.

I remember the jungle
sleeping in the gangster's basement
the black sand beach
acid in my stomach for days.
A woman brought me my meals
and I pointed a gun at the sun.
He said *you like the hand that feeds you*
you lick the hand that beats you
make yourself do it or it never gets done.

Flapper Cleopatra/Princess Tiny Cars

Over and over   this quick-dry wish for memory winter
is mainly fireproof
fatal woman freight hopping   the harder they come
asbestos snow.
The man's a different person at night
like a side piece to the moon landing
and my moral compass is low.

Xmas trees burn all year long on Archer Heights
but I only go out once in my courthouse suit
in my long veil and bones
then I come home
light up all my polyester nighties
my high-fashion dresses   light up
when the rich bachelor sends
the cardboard candy tower that collapses.

The marsh is different from the lake.
Animals seem tantamount
when you're rowing the canoe
my shiny, shiny hair
a peekaboo placebo.   I let you brother drown
with the ladders in my stockings
and the lily of the valley.
I lie that I don't leave
my hotel room open
only think of silent Hollywood.

Canary murder cherry bumper
sad fish at the cannery
over and over I plan my death
double whammy sleeping pills
fire under Frisco
roadster running in the garage.

There are too many cold trails
to take off my jewelry.
I shove the dresser   in front of the vanity.
They say give up when you're in a b-movie
but I don't have to listen
I just jump out the window.

JUNK
HANNAH

MOOD
NEAL

we never
have
the space
to fuck
there is
a chasm
between
my ocean
your farmland
it is coal plants

the air
in this city
is bearable
only because i
want it to be
for you
i want to journey
through heteroland
on my high horse
in the rain
squeezing my thighs
like a rodeo champ
while i hold
the umbrella
over
your head

the way you taste a fog
in New York City
is either too much
or not enough
the phrase alone:
skimmed off the tip

if you want
spontaneity
you can have
every
flavor
of exhaustion
sex and milky
discharge stuck
to your dick for all
the pillows
and dreams
i missed
if you want
consistency
you can always
leave like faulty
clockwork
the bar owner's
boyfriend
who is an artist
coined the phrase
"junk mood"
told me

crystal we could hit the road
crash into metal
forget the impact it was
brief and for the rest
of our neverending story
we met on the internet

you
materialized
the man
in white linen
to ask "who made you?"
and teach
a lesson
in pirouettes
on stilts
over
the brooklyn
bridge
what an impos-
sibility it is
to mind
the gap

heels sinking
faster
than my head
at 6am
under our
breath
we watch
firefighters
disappear
into the mouth
of the greasy
white
clouds

The blue oyster sunset at the dancing inn

We ran down broken
escalators entangled
our feet and made
echoes like shine
on tin, though light
was a dusty stained
glass tinge. It made a swarm
of you, all around me. Though
unwanted, comforting you
were steadfast
in footprints.

The escalator glitched.
You were led to a ship
yard with thousands of dead clams.
I couldn't fathom the depths.

Sure
plots twist, notes go sour
but why is it
that one minute you're dancing through a tunnel
and at the end you are a fishmonger living
in my recollected harbor raising dead clams
up from the water instead of children?

Sometimes you hear cries coming
from the inn though it's long abandoned
by the humans that renovated it.
They didn't intend
to die there. You used
to memorize phone numbers. Now, it seems
that letters keep
getting smaller more
frequent and divided. Your eyes
won't adjust
to the bigger picture.

You didn't intend to die here.
You cast your net

against a concrete block. It hits.
The pixels slink down without grasping
at anything. The ocean is a familiar.
You cannot tell whether it is moving.
You cannot resuscitate it.
You cannot recall the dance
of lines and fishermen.
The blue oyster cannot recall a time when
it was not blue. You wait, but there will be no great wave
to mask its face.

Portrait of a donut as a young hole

Wrapped in sugar, I cried into myself until I tasted salt.
Donut shops are disappearing behind lesbian bars because no one
likes eating their Wheaties anymore there are too many holes
to be filled and the holes that needed filling were already full.

This kid on her $1 shit wants
to sit on the cake where he eats it.

You taught me
to include the constellations
and in my attempt I scattered
powdered sugar in honor of past patterns.

You've come to know the tunnel
inside of me better than anyone:
how deep it goes, what could be scraped off,
wanderlust as a substitute
for spelunking for the moments where
your mouth fills with soft and supple
and it is uncomfortable

slow your roll.
Chew with your teeth.

I've traveled as a party of one
hour sleep to sit on a bench brown
paper bag blanket without you
and it is truly a mouthful of morning.

I don't even read the ads
on the subway it is just my reality
not paying attention, no storage capacity.

Missing from center like I've
been hit by an expert dart player too many times
or mauled by a bear. I remember having desire

to be both Robin Hood and the masses instead
I got stuck floating in the wave pool at Six Flags.
When I returned, years later,
the e-coli had frozen over.
It was special, and so
I wrote

> *How to Find Life: the frozen androgens*
> *hunched over time tubes and inner rafts*
> *with Blue Tooths.*

If I were to return again: free donuts
even for those who have trespassed.
Nothing like catching flies with sugar
        I mean friends
I mean until they bite down and discover
you contain salt after all that is the hardest practice.
No matter how many chemicals are in the application
you can never be truly fresh and you will always be
accountable for your ingredients.

I cried into myself
because I have a hole to fill.
The flakes will pass through my airways
and I will be reminded of your huge fake blueberry gaze,
how you stole my OxyContin just by standing next to me.

I needed it to breathe in this sobering century
both enlightenment and second coming.
I'll even take the bench with me so I can bench myself as
needed.
You will sit beside me and critique my glaze I'd like that
I think. Sometimes you just start thinking.

I'd like to thank Jesus for not
shaving me and the anonymity afforded
by New York City so that I could
lend my unique perspective to this particular and
completely unshared loneliness.

YOUR BODY HAS TO GO SOMEWHERE
EMELIA STEENEKAMP

And here is you, in this modern age, saying things like 'good morning,' and 'so it goes,' and 'my back hurts.' Here is you, standing in line to buy something that you think your mother might like. Here is you, probably in your late twenties, too old to be as stupid as you are.

In this modern world you have a job, and so you tell children things about the world according to a carefully curated selection of knowledge: it varies in temperature, it shuffles its parts around, and it's been doing its thing for a while now. There are times, however, when you find yourself to be nothing more than an abstraction of memory, worry, and undefined aches, making you doubt the concept of pastness, making you doubt that anything at all could be confirmed. You are not convinced that you really are here, but you have no choice other than to operate as if you are. Giving up is harder than playing along, because your body will always force you to keep going even when that means as little as finding a place to put it. Your body has to go somewhere.

In this modern world you have a job, and so you write papers according to a carefully curated language that channels your ideas into places you don't understand or agree with. Your holy mission is to articulate and substantiate your beliefs. But the modes and ideals of the institution shape them into products that feel foreign to you. Your work becomes smug and overdetermined. You always want to go home.

In this modern world you have a job, and so you film weddings according to a carefully curated selection of ideals concerning togetherness, community, and love. You document behaviour from strange lands and combine it with music to tether it to time and (some kind of purported) reality. On Saturday nights when you are tired you arrive home saturated with wedding songs and vicarious drunkenness, a dance floor and the onslaught of percussion that you did not like but could imagine liking in lighter air. Except for a few tiny insects and yourself, sitting on your bed with cold food and your shoes still on, the house is empty. The people you live with are elsewhere: in intimate situations, feeling their hands and hair move in newly alluring ways. You, on the other hand, are looking at people's lives on the internet and fixating on the problem of your second virginity, a miracle bestowed on you not by the White American God, but by time. You have been virgined by four years of lugging an unacceptable body which you have to pretend to be at peace with.

'Love your body,' read captions to online pictures upon which others bestow all the hearts and hands at their disposal.

> 'All bodies are beautiful!' you concur.
> 'It is a modern age,' they say.
> 'sluts are cool!'
> 'assholes are fun!'
> 'cum butter and so on.'

What they do not say is that everyone knows that you are faking it because your self-loathing exudes a smell of stale oil and bedsweat, making your true feelings impossible to hide. So despite them nodding when you say 'all bodies are beautiful,' or smiling when you wear things that are not made for people who look like you, they can smell you and what you really are, and they don't want to be near you in that way. You know how they feel and this knowledge exacerbates your odour and the sensation of live mincemeat under your skin. Whoever you are and however you might live, the thing about your life is that you try to get away from ugliness, only to find yourself relentlessly enveloped in it.

So you are a virgin again, and virginity is unacceptable for a person who claims emancipation. There has got to be someone who will have sex with you, who either believes it when they say 'all bodies are beautiful,' or who is lonely enough to betray themselves. You can find such people via the advanced sex relief application, as you are informed by an advertisement that features an attractive heterosexual couple shining in clean bohemian colours. Based on the things people say, as well as the part of the internet that's all about agency and orgasms, you know that your meat would be less horrid if only someone would want your body. So you pay $$$ to sign up for the service, and make an appointment for the included assessment and portrait assembly.

On some morning soon after this, three doctors come in gloves and white-coated radiance to your house to set up your self-promotion portrait. They are to examine you in the bathroom. You stand on the toilet, one doctor works from inside the shower, and the other two are pressed against the wall. You are impressed by how well they manoeuvre their tools and bodies in this small space.

1. 'Lift your arms.' You lift your arms.
2. 'Take off your clothes.' You take off your clothes.
3. 'Open your mouth.' You open your mouth.
4. 'Spread your legs.' You spread your legs.
5. 'Rub your clit.' You rub your clit.

Things made of steel or plastic or wood are placed in your nostrils, ears, vagina, belly button, asshole, mouth. You worry that the doctors can smell your angry smell, so you try to distract them by complimenting their professionalism. 'Thank you. We pride ourselves in conducting a thorough investigation of every client,' they say. You think surely many of their clients smell worse than you do.

They ask if they may sit down to analyse the data, and you say of course! if they don't mind sitting on your bed. They do mind but there are no other options, so they set up their computers on your duvet and pillows while you try to stop your bleeding and make jujube tea for everyone. You place the tea on the middle of the bed where the doctors are frowning together at something on a screen. They are unhappy about the screen but they like the tea. While frowning-smiling-sipping with thin erudite fingers, they tell you that your body produces too much black bile, which is why you are lazy. For [money] they could perform bloodletting therapy on you (sip). You say no thank you. Maybe next month. They ask if you want to make a video to introduce yourself to potential sex friends. It costs only E3,44M. No thanks, you say, you cannot afford it.

Then you fill out a seventeen page questionnaire, indicating your preferences regarding colours and food, and answering questions like 'where were you when you first realised that you will never get the things you want from life?' and 'have you ever been sexually attracted to a family member?'

The next step is to generate your bio and curate your photos. You have to provide the doctors with photos of yourself so that, with the help of carnal algorithms, they may select the ones most likely to entice a fellow sex-seeker.

You say that you need to check your garden's soil pH: 'I will be right back.' Outside, you take photos of your face, hoping to locate a part of yourself that isn't hideous. You settle for a picture that doesn't feature your chin. Then you compile another 26 taken over the past two years, photos your friends claimed to like. Of these, the doctors choose only two, including one in which you are hiking on a hill in the distance, almost looking like a normal person. For the other obligatory photo slots they take two pictures of your cat. They feed the photos into their computers, who now need a few minutes to think. Worried that they are bored, you put on some music. 'Do you like the carpenters?' you ask, but they seem annoyed at this question as if it is too personal. You make another round of tea, and they announce that your portrait is ready. Your bio reads as follows:

> anything, kinky non-belief or otherwise, natural sensual. off lick some the be for good humour. Have cynical, seem beautiful some relaxed. are are a interested in the fun, to lifestyle you brunettes blow You jungle wit is prefer in to where. very I anal steam white, sense travel please...

The doctors look proud of their work. They say that you may publish the portrait online as soon as you are ready to do so. They tell you that as it stands your desirability index (DI) is 3.2., which is on the low side but not at all rock bottom. There will be plenty of suitable options for you. But if you want to improve your DI, they say, you should pay for the video or sign up for their liposuction treatment. They could offer you a reduced rate of ¼4~7etc;). Thank you so much! but I can't afford it, you say. Maybe next month. They smile politely and leave in a straight line, their coats glorious white birds of peace.

Now, at 9pm, you are alone, and still leaking blood here and there. You are contorted on a corner of your bed, which is covered in lipstick-marked tea cups and spilt sugar. Sucking on a spoon, you upload your portrait and begin to use the programme. There are pictures of people doing adventure sports and drinking colourful liquids from curvy glasses, and videos of them having orgasms or shooting animals.

Person 1

S: licking white Stroke ass milk oily that sit flow on lips
You: we're die here. naughty all be.
B: anus me please with enjoy Friends your I please!!! Show
       benefits, vagina sweet that, don't wine
You: but Your to yes no lack

Here is one, talking in a bar. When they laugh, their eyes are
too much for your eyes and you have to look away. You drink.
Now they are on your bed with you and the teacups. She has
an erection and you are both shaking a bit. Your own body is
unyielding, so you sleep instead. In the early morning hours
you are both awake. She cries and tells you about her father on
a farm while you watch your cat making use of the litter box,
waiting for the smell to reach the bed and wondering what it
will do to the ghost of the father idling in the room. The spaces
between words grow bigger, and you and her and her ghost
dissipate into another uncomfortable sleep.

Person 2

You: hello please ja jou lekker sies
J: I'm open, bene vir kanne, while
                   sexually dirty your are No as. to ladies! not into
                   Sorry, might.
You: Drink shiny milk to three cans. The mountain is
                   bad. The wolf is screaming. I love hiking in the
                   chestnut valley. Bring vir my ietsie oulik van
                   Frankryk af.
J: sugar to pussy. naai vir dag na netso in ok. chill.
You: IM STRAWBERRIES FOR WET YOU PASSION
                   DO YOU UNDERSTAND

Here is one, talking in a bar. When they laugh their eye contact is too much for your eyes and you have to look at your hands. You drink something that makes your stomach hurt. Now they are on your bed with you and the teacups. You both know that you have to do the things. He puts his face on yours, and you fumble about together, dehydrated and disorganised, until you are dirty and raw and have essentially given up. Then you take some kind of drug together and talk about things like dead stars and war. The cat purrs at the window, you can hear it laughing as it plays with its tail. You float into that sleep in which it feels like you are awake.

Person 3

You: **나를 더 사랑해줘**
Person 3:   **이제 산에 오르자** jou ma is hier :0
You: **지금** imagine jy voel 'n actual konneksie met 'n
              ander mens vir eens in jou lewe**당장 정원 등을
              정비하다**
Person 3:   **나는 진짜가 되지 않을**in next for? TIETE

Here is one, talking in a bar. When they laugh their eye contact
is too much for your eyes and you have to look at your drink.
Now they are on your bed with you and the teacups. You wish
you had replaced the cat litter. You lie looking at your hands,
neither of you willing/able to do the things you came here to do.
You are both trembling a little, sad, nothing to say. Neither of you
understand what you want. You fall asleep holding each other.

While you sleep you have a headache. It hardens your skull so that nothing can come into it, the pain trapped like a discontented relative of the rest of your ugliness. So you have a dream in which you are free – bright yellow clothes mythical childhood etc. – but the freedom is on the outside of your head, circling your skull, finding no place to enter and eventually giving up and leaving in search of some other better skull.

After an unusual amount of time you wake up alone. You have menstruated on the sheets, the blood is cheerful in its fresh redness. You leave the sheets as they are, and pack your stomach medicine along with three changes of clothing. You walk outside and see hills appearing as you near them. After a while of nothing but semi-cubist landscape, you begin to pass ruins of factories, schools, prisons. You enter a building that used to house a printing press: rusted equipment abject and impotent; and you imagine the things that might have been printed there, what kind of allegiances they held, hoping that you would've liked them. There is something painfully sympathetic about rust and it seems rude to harbour ill will towards it even if it came to exist due to a terror of sorts. You walk up a flight of stairs to encounter a door that you are excited to open, but when you grab at the doorknob you hurt your nails against a wall, realising that the door has been printed onto it. Then you stand still for a while like a plant. Time passes and you realise that you are moving again, making your way back down the stairs and out of the building, where you continue to walk past further moments of corroded industry. A pile of shipping containers appeals to you, so you climb up and explore them one by one, finding medical supplies, canned food, expired condiments. In the topmost container you hear a foreign yelping sound coming from inside a cabinet. You touch the cabinet door and it opens to reveal a rhesus monkey. The monkey jumps out and clambers onto your breasts and tries to suckle. It is slightly delirious. There is a bottle of milk lying on the floor so you feed the monkey who, now satiated, climbs under your shirt and attaches itself to your belly. You hold it there and it falls asleep. Back on the ground you walk, monkey-under-shirt, towards the sounds of seagulls enjoying their freedom from gravity. Then the mountain stops. You see a beach below. After a few failed attempts you manage to safely hop down the cliff and onto the beach where the sound of the seagulls is loud even though can't seem to see them. You walk towards the water, but when you try to step into the waves you cannot. You hop up and down against it, not really thinking that it will relent but, having been betrayed by a false promise, you are feeling too dejected for much else and dissenting in a way that doesn't demand too much of you.

Then you discover yourself to be walking along the beach. The monkey has disappeared. A jagged hill is approaching. When it arrives, you see a small cave. You go inside and you find the monkey curled sweetly on a single bed. And now here is you, sobbing quietly in a little cave with white linen, a bookshelf, and a hole that lets you look at the sky. You and the monkey lie softly weaved together; you need the monkey as much as it needs you. Your needy limbs melt into one another until you become a blanket and you know that a blanket is the perfect thing to be and that you will never need anything but to be a blanket forever.

END OF TERM EXAM
MARIA   GREER

1. If Train A leaves the station at 8:45, heading due east
    at seventy-five miles per hour, and Train B leaves the
    station twenty-eight minutes later, going ninety in the
    opposite direction, which one will you be on?

2. There's a man on Train B who wants to kill you. I know
    this and he knows this and you know this. None of us
    knows just how or when he'll do it—
    a) poison at midnight
    b) car crash at dawn
    c) cancer at forty-five
    but we know he won't give up until you're cold in the
    ground.

3. You met him a long time ago and you keep going back
    to him, because he's promised you death and you kind
    of admire his honesty. He wears a false ▯ mustache but
    his teeth are true ▯.

4.

x	1	2	3	4	5
1	I'm	waiting	at	the	station
2	where	Train	A	gets	in.
3	I	don't	know	what	time
4	it's	supposed	to	arrive.	
5	I	forgot	my	times	tables.

5. The woman (w) standing next to me at the station (s)
    has the system map (m) tattooed on her forearm (f). She
    doesn't ride anymore, unless you count buses (b). Solve
    for t (train).

6. I thought your train might have gotten here by now, muscling into the station the way my father always did, as though we were waiting on him, as though we would always be happy to see him—but neither you nor I have ever been the muscling type. Maybe that's our problem. We always wanted to know what our problem is so maybe that's it. Underline the problem.

7. I'm waiting. Take your time. I'll just sit here [quickly/ quiescently/quietly].

8a. Which of the following describes Train A? (Choose all that apply.)
   ☐ cheap
   ☐ rusty
   ☐ falling apart
   ☐ will bring you to me

8b. Which of the following describes Train B? (Choose all that apply.)
   ☐ will take you straight off a cliff

9. I want you to get on Train A, but I don't want to beg. Write a short persuasive essay arguing in favor of Train A.

10. I lied. Please let me _____.
   ○ beg
   ○ take you home
   ○ drink from your neck
   ○ press fingerprints into your skin
   ○ pour chalky pastel hearts down your throat

11. Back to the man on Train B. He keeps looking at his watch, which is _____ (adjective), because we all know his train left at _____ (time) and is traveling at exactly the speed it will take to kill _____ (pronoun).

12. Match subject with object:

You   are going to him anyway.
I   know you are.
We   all hate the way you look at him,
that man   and his jellyfish smile.
He   wants to swallow you whole.
To be honest, darling, so do   I.

13. Fix the errors in the following sentence:
    Its 11:45 and I'm waiting for you're train to get
    in, but you're now coming.

14. Diagram the following sentence:
    I think it but I don't feel it, like when you stub your toe
    on the baseboard, and there's a moment when your
    brain just thinks, Oh, this is going to really hurt in just a
    second—and then, yes, you're right, it hurts, way to go,
    Einstein, you predicted the pain.

15a. Does that make you feel any better?

15b. Does that make you say I told you so?

16. So you told me. You told me you were going to give me
    pain, and I didn't _____.

```

```

17. Throw up the candy hearts. Order them sequentially (1-5). Give them back.

        __ U R CUTE
        __ B MINE
        __ I LUV U
        __ I MISS U
        __ TTFN

Answer key:

1.Train A leaves the station at 8:45
2.heading due east
3.at seventy-five miles per hour.
4.Train B leaves the station twenty-eight minutes later
5.going ninety
6.in the opposite direction, and
7.you're on it.
8.Stop trying to deny it.
9.You know that man will be the death of you
10.and you don't care anymore, because
11.it feels safer, because
12.you always liked the taste of poison.
13.I love you more than he does, you know.
14.I wish you'd let me kill you
15.instead.
16.a) false
17.b) true

STOP WRITING EPIC POEMS ABOUT MY DICK, YOU FREAK!
SHANE ALLISON

Stop writing epic poems about my dick, you freak
Stop writing epic poems about my dick,
You freak. Stop writing epic poems
About my dick, you
Freak. Stop writing epic
Poems about my

Dick, you freak. Stop writing epic poems about my
Dick, you freak. Stop writing epic poems about my dick, you
freak
Stop writing epic
Poems about my dick,
You freak. Stop writing epic poems about my dick, you
Freak. Stop writing epic poems

About my dick, you freak. Stop writing epic poems
About my dick, you freak. Stop writing epic poems about my
Dick, you freak. Stop writing epic poems about my dick, you
Freak. Stop writing you freak ,
Epic poems about my dick,
You freak. Stop writing epic

Poems about my dick, you freak. Stop writing epic
Poems about my dick, you freak. Stop writing poems
Epic about my dick,
You freak. Stop writing epic poems about my
Dick, you freak.
Stop writing epic poems about my dick, you

Freak. Stop writing epic poems about my dick, you
Freak. Stop writing, you freak, epic
Poems about my dick, you freak.
Stop writing epic poems
About my dick, you freak. Stop writing epic poems about my
Dick, you freak. Stop writing epic poems about my dick,

You freak. Stop writing epic poems, you freak, about my dick.
Stop writing epic poems about my dick, you
Freak. Stop writing epic poems about my
Dick, you freak. Stop writing epic
Poems about my dick, you freak. Stop writing epic poems
About my dick, you freak.

Stop writing epic
Poems about my
Dick, you freak.

LITTLE HOMOSEXUAL IN GREEN

This was not the homosexual I envisioned
Free to all the lead-poisoned, mindful of sodomy in closet
desperation
First-class homosexuals they, though with sinewy clutch,
(An unyielding clench). They promised to never wax my staff

Free to all the lead-poisoned, mindful of sodomy in closet
desperation
I promised to aggravate it upon request while shoving the
homsexual
(An unyielding clench.) They promised to never wax my staff
Of flags in my eye, lovely masses of untrained homosexuals

I promised to aggravate it upon request while shoving the
homosexuals
In the debts of my soul. A little homosexual in green eats hope
Of flags in my eye. Lovely masses of untrained homosexuals
Is painterly. Stuff amends in your eyes. Praise the homosexuals
multiplying

In the debts of my soul. A little homosexual in green eats hope
In the head-eating ear wax the envoys. I quadrupled, duty-bound
Is painterly. Stuff amends in your ears. Praise the homosexuals
multiplying.
Let the arts free homosexuals from the shackles of habit

In the head-eating ear wax the envoys. I quadrupled, duty-bound
I have not swam across great theories in the presence of a loose
Transsexual. Let the arts-free homosexuals from the shackles of
habit knot touch
Me, so I am free to free homosexuals

I have not swam across great theories in the presence of a loose
Coin-operated drag queen. I, with no quintessential homosexual
habit
Knot touch me, so I am free to free homosexuals
Free to form opinions on their own and transfix what needs to be
transfixed.

WHITE MALE FOR WHITE MALE

Where's all the action?
I'm new.
Looking for a good cock suck.
I'm alone in my dorm,
Wearing red, satin boxers,
Needing my dick sucked.
I'm a hot white male looking for other hot white males
I'm new to this place.
I was in the bathroom on the second floor of Strozier Library
Looking for guys to suck my cock.
Where's the action?
I'm alone.
When is a good time?
I'm new in town.
White and hard,
Loves to suck,
Loves to get sucked.
White male wearing red satin boxers.
Be here at eleven p.m.
I'm alone in my dorm.
I need my dick sucked.
Where's the action?
White man will suck you dry.
This is all new to me.
You won't be disappointed.
White guys only.
White cock only.
I'm alone wearing red boxers, satin.
I need my balls drained.
Let me know if you're cool.
Let's meet up.
I'm in my dorm.
Where are the hot spots for hot cock?
White male for white males.
I'm new to this.
You won't be disappointed.

C I R C L I N G
THE   BLOCKS
APRIL   SOPKIN

The end approached, but dailiness is dailiness. Sustaining.

My alarm went off at six, though some days it was five, the early hour meant for finishing homework. I slipped from bed, a thirty-one-year-old undergraduate, serious and intentional, my timetable exhaustively compartmentalized between classes, part-time job, and home. My boyfriend of six years slept on in the bed, having worked a late shift at one of his three jobs. Jeremy. Often, I was asleep before he came home from work, and his own alarm had yet to go off by the time I left for campus.

That morning, like every morning, I made myself as quiet as possible.

It was almost spring, but the cold was trapped in our enormous railroad apartment, and I pulled a heavy sweater over my pajamas. I tip-toed, tried to avoid the floorboards that gave way noisily. At my desk in the high-ceilinged front room with the vibrant yellow walls, I stretched my numb toes, and tried but could not focus on my homework. The boy cat meowed once from the floor, waiting for the milk dregs from my cereal bowl. I could hear Jeremy, in bed, as he shifted and the other cat, the girl, squawked at him.

I stared at my laptop, at the walls, at nothing. A vague escalation of panic, like the same note being tapped out on a piano in another room, except the room was somewhere inside of me.

Six years was the longest relationship of my life. Of Jeremy's life, too. We met on an island in Maine where he was assisting the author leading the writing workshop I was attending. The boat had pulled up to the shore, and Jeremy waited there on the dock, very tall, in a plaid button-down, yellow-blonde curls fluffed by the humidity. He told me later, when he saw me for the first time, he thought, *Oh shit.*

Who could abandon an origin story like that?

These mornings were so quiet that I could hear, from blocks away, the elderly man who shuffled his feet through the neighborhood on a daily jog. His sneakers never left the ground, and it was the scraping of the cement that I heard. I stood, leaned over my desk, pulled the blinds apart as I waited for him to pass my building, same as the day before, such painstaking progress. After, I put on my coat and shoes and quietly left the house.

Two blocks away, I picked up a coffee then bought a pack of cigarettes at the market. Unofficially, I'd been smoking again for months—the first inhale offering a rush of relief so shamefully welcome and deliciously secretive that, briefly, all my problems disappeared. Then I walked. The problems came back. It was a beautiful day, it was never about the weather, and my exhaustion had nothing to do with being tired. These secret walks were deliberately slow, and my thoughts circled as I circled blocks. I felt deeply restless, and fearful of the growing sense that, waiting on the other side of these quiet mornings and our opposite schedules, was a reckoning in our relationship that I would be responsible for.

At some point in the past year, I'd fallen out of love with the person I'd planned to spend my life with. I walked. I came to terms. I walked more. Down Robinson to Stuart, down Mulberry to Floyd, up Davis and back to Stuart. In my throat was cigarette smoke, was a twitching readiness to cry, was a controlled deep breath instead of the things I couldn't yet say aloud. These things I couldn't yet say lingered in the periphery of my mind, but all the gaps were narrowing, soon the periphery would be brought dead center.

Every relationship is a particular world yet sketched with universal familiarity. That Jeremy and I fell in love and grew apart is not unusual, that he didn't want to get married and I did is nothing new, that money was always a problem, that we rarely fought and, thus, rarely laid things bare, that the future was perpetually about next week and never next year, no, none of this, at all, is any sort of unique lightning strike of the unforeseen.

Every year there were presents for him under the Christmas tree at my mother's house. The same for me at his parents'. All the traveling: Berlin, Boston, Prague, Cannon Beach, Seattle, Austin, Toronto. What did a person *do* with all the photos of our faces together? Simply for that reason, I could not walk away. It seemed illogical to even think it—our faces! Together! In so many photos!

What happens to documented personal history when its presumed future is abandoned? What happens to those people we thought we'd become together?

For much of the duration of our relationship, specifically as the years started to mount, I would test these questions. The hypothetical break-up projected easily in my mind—not what caused it, rather only the fact of it: our separateness, our severance, the time accumulated now wasted. In my gut, as I imagined the end, I always felt the floor dropping out, followed by an undefined and abstract blankness. That was all. Because I could not actually imagine the content of my life in our aftermath. I couldn't imagine starting over.

This inability to imagine, I took for years as a positive sign about the relationship.

When one person senses the end, and the other does not, that's the discrepancy I was carrying alone on these secret, early morning walks around my neighborhood. The discomfort of knowing the future, of being the one who sees what can't be fixed, of the incremental shift over time from love to questioning to arriving on the other side of a threshold. I walked. Down Robinson to Stuart, down Mulberry to Floyd, up Davis and back to Stuart. I felt the threshold behind me, a line that never moved, only I moved away from it, faster now with the realization that I'd even crossed it at all.

It was devastating yet somehow thrilling, the loneliness of knowing the end was getting closer. Of encountering that abstract blankness. Of imagining myself entering into it. I was raw emotion on these walks, vibrating from nicotine, caffeine, fear, cold. Eventually, for months after the break-up, I would arrive at rage, toward myself and Jeremy combined, a recurrent desire to blame someone for the wasted years and the dashed expectations. My therapist likened this anger phase to the second stage of grief. I was so filled with rage that I had trouble sleeping, my body flushing with adrenaline during those spare nighttime moments, thoughts racing backward toward the end, over and over.

We loved each other via the undemanding inertia of having loved each other for a long time. We loved each other via unthinking routine, allegiance, expectation. We loved each other via all the days that pass without notice, via the way people pragmatically require each other in a financial sense, via one person's explicit emotional needs being always stronger than the other's ability to speak plain and be heard.

People fall out of love for many reasons. This isn't about the reasons.

On these walks, my thoughts shifted from the initial exigency of how to retrieve what was lost, and, instead, began to consider how to extricate myself from what was done. The distinction felt criminal. I would need a place to stay in the interim. I would need to ask my brother for money. I would need to pick up more shifts, immediately. I walked. I breathed. I smoked.

How is it that impending destruction can feel so strangely hopeful, can feel so right?

Before these plans could be put in place, before the rage that came along later, before the end was articulated in a shaky voice one night after dinner, there was first the warmth of a cup of coffee against my palm on those early frigid mornings just before the spring. There was another turn down another block. There was a spot in the center of my chest, quivering, as the past six years crushed together like a reverse Big Bang. There was me, alone, circling, as I worked things through. As I came to terms. As I started to lean into my heart's new separateness, where I was already alone, on my own, and practicing it. |

ELVIS CLONE
BOUNTY HUNTERS
JACQUES DEBROT

The trio of Elvises lip-synching on YouTube to a bonzo hip-hop version of "Love Me Tender" are illegals.

"Look at that," Ugly Romeo says, pointing to this awkward thing the clones do mid-song where they break into a flurry of karate moves. It's the fourth video the Elvis clones have uploaded this week.

"Turtle-Sticks-Its-Head-Out," Yo-Yo jokes. "Seven-Fang-Terror-Smash." She and Romeo terminate Elvis illegals weekly on their hit reality-TV show, but they're both superfans of the King. Yo-Yo's even got Elvis's death date, 8-16-1977, tattooed on the roof of her mouth.

Romeo zooms in on a Chinese watermark barely visible beneath a sweaty, wedge-shaped sideburn. "This is sick," he says, pressing the zoom button combination again. By now Romeo's so used to having every minute of his life recorded that he's only remotely aware of the S&M Network cameraman filming him for the show. "It's like these Elvises are just asking us to waste them."

"WTF, how can you watch this crap?" Sticky Fingaz asks. "Ugly Romeo is such a shithat."

For the past ten minutes, she's been enumerating Poster Boy's inadequacies as a boyfriend, but he just shrugs indifferently like he's high, both eyes glued to his laptop.

"I thought we were going out tonight."

"Go then," Poster Boy says in a tone of surly boredom. "What do I care?"

The camera closes in on Romeo as he plays the clone video for Psylocke and Young Elephant Man.

"What do you make of this?" he asks. He pauses the video and hits the Select button, enlarging one of the Elvises' bloated features.

"Close in on the sunglasses," Psylocke suggests. She and Young Elephant Man are Romeo's grown kids from his first marriage. Yo-Yo's about their age so sometimes the family dynamic gets weird. Plus, the kids are mutants. Psylocke sees people as colors, like her mom, shimmering purples, dull greens.

Young Elephant Man takes control of the keyboard and zeroes in on the clone's chunky gold aviator sunglasses. As he magnifies the left lens, the reflected image of a large disordered room comes into focus.

"It looks like an abandoned office," Psylocke says. "Disheveled cubicles, busted file cabinets."

Young Elephant Man zooms in again. "Watch this." A little pinwheel icon on the display spins and the view scrolls toward a window on the office's opposite wall. Suddenly a streetscape appears. The clone hunters are gazing out the window now. The detail is astonishing.

"The Venice Beach Ruins is my guess," Psylocke says.

Young Elephant Man hits the ZZ button again and the image of a collapsed freeway comes into view. Huge slabs of concrete tilted at extreme angles, twisted pilings. "That's Interstate 10, right?" A swatch of loose skin swings from the back of his skull. His gray head looks like a giant cauliflower. "We're a mile south of Washington Boulevard's my best guess."

Sticky Fingaz gets up off Poster Boy's bed in her bra and underwear and scrounges around the room for her clothes. The carpet's littered with dented cans of Fistfite Light, chip bags, and old takeout food containers. Sweeping aside a sticky box of General Tso's chicken, she accidentally tips over a glass bong.

"Hey man, be fucking careful," Poster Boy mumbles.

A title materializes on Poster Boy's laptop. THE VENICE BEACH RUINS, it says. A GUTTED OFFICE BUILDING INTERIOR.

"Hey jack, dig this," an Elvis in a white jumpsuit says. He plays a little riff on his beat-up Gibson.

"I like it, Boss," a second Elvis volunteers. Then he plays the riff back a little differently on his own instrument.

The two jam awhile, until a third Elvis clomps drunkenly into the room with a Smite & Waste'em 20/20. Something's gone haywire in his DNA. Left to his own devices he'll stay high for days and brood over true-seeming memories of his spurious past life— attending Bible classes as a child, the lost years in Germany, his alcoholic mother's death. Curling his lips in a nasty sneer, he plops down on a wobbly office chair. "You know, I could waste both you greasers right now," he says, "and do the world a big favor." He leans back and closes his eyes. His belly lies in his lap like a balloon full of water.

Sticky Fingaz pokes her arm under Poster Boy's bed like a contortionist, finds her smartphone half-shirt and gaze-actuated leggings, and pulls them on. "Laters," she says, pausing at the door.

Onscreen the TV bounty hunters put their hover cars down on the Elvis hideout's scorched rooftop. It's high tide. What's left of Venice is drowned under three feet of seawater. Ugly Romeo flips down his clip-on helmet cam. There's a UV alert for the fifth straight day and the clone hunters are all cooking in their heavy body armor, messy sweat dripping down their back and legs like pond scum. The sky, bright with glowing red smog, resembles a photograph of bubbling lava.

In no time, they locate a stairwell bulkhead behind a pair of rusted-out turbine vents. Romeo kicks the door open with his boot and Yo-Yo, Psylocke, and Young Elephant Man fall in behind, battle choppas drawn.

Poster Boy hits the pause button on his laptop. "What?" he asks Sticky Fingaz over his shoulder. "You're still here?"

Turning abruptly to the camera mounted on Romeo's helmet, Psylocke's eyes go wide. She raises a hand in warning. "You hear that?" she asks. Of course, Psylocke herself doesn't actually "hear" anything in the ordinary sense. Instead, she perceives a shifting amoebic-like field of psychedelic colors.

Yo-Yo and Young Elephant Man stop to listen. The wormy blue veins in Young Elephant Man's cauliflower head begin to pulsate. From someplace deep in the foul-smelling building below comes the faint recorded whine of "Suspicious Minds."

Sticky Fingaz flashes Poster Boy the bird. "Fuck you," she says.

The room the clone hunters enter is a maze of overturned desks. Yo-Yo catches sight of a huge shape materializing in the murk. "My God," she whispers. It's a levitating Elvis Head the size of fifty basketballs. Abruptly the music stops, replaced a second later by the opening fanfare from "Thus Spoke Zarathustra."

Sticky Fingaz's pulling ferociously on the handle, but Poster Boy's door won't open. "Alexa, open the fucking door," she demands. "Now."

"I went to Hollywood," the Head intones as the Zarathustra intro ebbs away. "My next move was to Hollywood. I was twenty-one. That's how it works. You get a record and then you get on television and then they take you to Hollywood to make movies." The Head seems confused. "I don't feel I'll live a long life," it continues tentatively. "That's why I got to get what I can."

In frustration, Sticky Fingaz kicks the door hard. It judders around in its frame.

"I'm sorry, I'm having trouble understanding," Alexa says.

Now the hologram or whatever it is disappears and the clone hunters hear the CHUNG-chung of a twelve-gauge Street

Sweeper being activated. It's the nasty-tempered Elvis, big as a bear on its hind legs.

KAPOW! A round slams into the wall behind them. Then another.

Yo-Yo does an athletic back handspring in retreat as Romeo hits the deck awkwardly before letting go with his Warhammer. The first slug catches the clone in the forehead. His cranium goes pyroclastic.

"Gross," Sticky Fingaz exclaims.

The clone remains upright for a second. Then, falling to his knees, topples over, spraying blood in a fountainy arc.

Finally, Poster Boy's door unbolts with a soft chiming noise. Unfortunately, once again the elevator's out of service so Sticky Fingaz shakily descends ten flights of stairs in her glitter thigh-highs. She's drenched with sweat when she steps outside. As she makes her way to the subway station, she can feel the sun's weight pressing down on her body.

Young Elephant Man spots the IED first—a long section of PVC pipe bristling with wires. His misshapen jaw drops. "Bomb," he shouts. "Everybody, out of here."

"Spare me some change?" a Young Elvis sitting Indian-style on a cardboard box asks Sticky Fingaz. He's wearing a rockabilly bowling shirt and torn jeans. A hypodermic syringe lies next to his swollen feet. He stares at Sticky Fingaz with fierce blue eyes and holds out a black-nailed hand. But Sticky Fingaz's broke so she pushes on toward the subway platform. There, she encounters more homeless Elvises. Fat, Young, all kinds. Huddled under a fluorescent light, a "Comeback" Elvis in a greasy black leather suit shares a bottle with a "Movie Years" clone. The clone, who looks like he just stepped off the set of *Girls! Girls! Girls!*, takes a long wincing gulp, then goes into a coughing fit. Behind them, an obese "Las Vegas" Elvis lies passed out on a graffiti-covered bench.

Young Elephant Man's warning comes too late. In a blinding heat blast, the bomb explodes. Monster billows of smoke and flame leap out like dragons and fill the room. Seconds pass. Nothing moves. Then the echoey sound of "Return to Sender" is heard playing on a scratching speaker, but far away and strange-feeling, like it's not even real. Like nothing is.

DISGUSTING
CHARLENE ELSBY

John and I used to spend all of our time together. For years, nothing could separate us, as much as could be helped. We would arrange things that way. It was obvious. It was always to be. When one exchanges molecules with the same person, day in and day out, it's as if they begin to work together, to impulse the flesh along a certain course of action, and ours always put us together. If ever we were apart for too long, it seemed as if the universe were doing us an injustice, and it had to be corrected. We would joyously come together again, exulting in our having deflated the scornful attempts of nature to part us, when one cannot part singular substance. When things grow apart, they say, they evolve differently. They adapt to their environments and slowly become nothing but strangers, things that maintain the material remnants of the one thing they used to be. I suppose you could say that we had a common ancestor.

In November, I put on an outer skin and so did he. It always seemed unfair that his outer skins could be layered, while mine were expected not to be. There were some things that were not mine—my neck, my arms, my upper back. These were everyone else's fleshes. I was happy for the evening, as it seemed to me as if the elasticity preserving our unity was slackening. There was no tension in between our beings, nothing taut, and it seemed as if to pull it would only slacken it more. So the fact that we were to go together, I thought, would do something to strengthen our mixture.

The trouble with a human doll is that you can *not* see behind the eyes, not even if you wanted to. It turns out that behind them is just more flesh—not what I wanted to see. I wanted to see their vision, their purposiveness. As if their gaze stopped short several inches from me, their glassiness looked as if it were shining to distract me, whereas they used to shine just as if to shine. I would look in the direction of the glare and then nothing. They would use the opportunity to pull away from me, everything going with them. Then, I knew, that was how I got in. It had something to do with the alignment of our gaze that allowed for the proper exchange of materials, and by looking away he meant to deny me.

He was largely silent on the way over. I had gotten used to it. It used to be that everything that happened, everything that was, was so in exacting detail. He wanted me to see as he saw and to know everything he knew, and that would ensure our mutual alignment. When I noticed his words were shorter than usual, I said it was for no reason at all. When I noticed that it was always that way, I noticed it always. When I see him across the table now, I don't think he's looked me in the eye for several months. He used to keep it up, for the sake of appearances, but at some point it was no longer allowed. There was something so final about it, as if it weren't the case that he could simply look at me and do away with all of the chewing, the swallowing and swirling, the torment of that mass inside him. I just knew that he would never look at me again, and that was that.

After the way over, that was when it was. He would look in a direction, and I would try to follow his gaze, and nothing. There was nothing there, nothing to feed on, nothing to find. It was as if he'd picked an angle at which to look and this was the least offensive one. This angle could not be questioned. Of course, when the others came, everything seemed as it were.

We were seated at a middle table and though I preferred the side, it was far enough away from the other tables that it wouldn't be a problem. I can't stand it when someone turns their back to you, and who knows what's getting on your backside, whether it's hair or skin or some putrid saliva from someone's loud laughter when it always seemed that what they were laughing about is how they were invading my flesh sack. That metaphor doesn't work. There's no hole at the top to make the truth out of it.
We were joined by several other people, and John seemed happy. He was speaking about the things he knew about, and

the people seemed to know also what he knew about, and they were also happy. The lights came down from above like umbrellas brought inside, with the topside down to let the water drain off. We stayed dry, and the laughter all around came in hot waves, comforting exchanges of dry warmth, building upon one another. With my neck exposed, I felt that in order to get at it, one would have to swim through the wafts of laughter before ramming in their jagged blades. Some dignity I would have if my air tubes leaked prematurely, and soaked in a blood rider hitching along with the quick release of wind from my churning innards, ruining the evening.

I knew all along that it would have to end, and I thought through the many scenarios we could have on the way home, when nothing was left of them. Perhaps their air would remain, and John would keep up with it, breaking through the distance angle. Perhaps not.

I was on John's left, and she was on his right, and what I saw was a hand and a leg in close juxtaposition. Without seeming too obvious, I took a measurement of their distance and, leaving no room for uncertainties, checked the angles of my gaze. Were I farther down, were I several inches shorter, perhaps a foot, I would be able to see if there were space in between the leg and the hand and the fingers, even though I knew that I would not see it, because the angles simply weren't right. They were all over the place, those fingers, glancing at the inside of the thigh as if they lived there, belonged there. The angles could not work, because the hand was so arrogantly positioned *around* the leg, and at once I felt a separation from the table as if I knew I didn't belong there and so did they. I was, all of a sudden, cut off like a gangrenous limb, and the body goes on all the better for it, never wondering where the leg ended up or how it was doing. Because it was dead.

I looked at John, and he didn't look at me. I was a corpse brought round. She didn't look at me either, or even at John. There wasn't anywhere to look at all, it turned out, and it didn't matter how one tried the angles.

That was November and now it is not. From there I could see it developing frighteningly quickly. As the living parts of our organism carried on, they garnered strength from an input that didn't even seem to be possible, but somehow it did. Through the layers of artifice and skin flesh and must, it seemed to be most obvious. I didn't have to look at him anymore to know what his face was doing. It was evident enough. Eat your bloody bread, John. They use the word "visceral" too often, but never does it mean what it's supposed to mean, and that's always disappointing.

I can hear the moisture coming out of his gums and soaking the bread. It lands hollow in the side of his face and becomes engulfed in flesh. It doesn't dissolve. It would be nice if it dissolved. It does not.

It converts to a flesh-covered meal that's slowly soaked in well-stewed saliva that's been marinating his teeth until they too seem soft, but still hard enough. He squishes the air out with his smacking around, taking the air from the spongy bread and centrifuging it out, leaving a soaked mass of yeasty meal on the one side of his mouth and an air pocket on the other, part of it in a pendulous swing of inhales and exhales. He breathes through his mouth while he's eating. The other part of the air escapes, and it's too hard to smell even from here.

When it's small enough to swallow and all of the flavor has been sucked out, dissipating through vessels here and there, the wasted mass seems to disappear from view, but I can still see it. It works its way down the pipe next to the air hole and swells it from the inside, a slide propelled by muscular contractions from the table to the gut. Looking through his face I can see it all writhing around in there. The bread doesn't dissolve. It's thrown about by fleshy masses that don't keep to themselves. They seem distinct and indistinct and all connected, full of refuse. It's disgusting. He didn't live off bread, but ate as one would eat if one were trying to convince another that one was alive, but he didn't need it to live. That's why it kept turning around in there, never melding.

I look at his arms. At least I've never had hairy arms, like some people, but they say it's all right for a man. It doesn't seem as if the bread ever gets there, but it must, or the arms would stop working. There would be nothing there to move them. Does it get there in the blood?

The blood would seep out if it weren't for the flesh and the flesh would fall off if it weren't all sealed, all the way around. You can't find a seam anywhere, not even at the tips of the fingers. Where did he start to make it? From the inside. It all works if you think of it from the inside first. There's a belly full of rotten pink snakes eating bread down there in the middle and everything shoots forth out of it. If you tear it apart, it doesn't look like the anatomy textbook. The anatomy keeps everything separate when in fact it's all mixed. It's all woven but not woven, more smushed up in there, so the organs have no choice but to cooperate. There's no room for fighting.

I try to picture all of the skin flakes he's left all over the house. There's no use trying to keep up with it. You can go from corner to corner and by the time I've gotten back around to the first there they are again. They live in the air and take my oxygen from it, rationing it back to me, meting it out in bits and pieces and pockets, as long as I keep getting the work done.

He sweats through his arms, and I used to hope that it would help the skin flakes stick to it better, that he would be more self-contained, but it doesn't. It just makes it stick to the carpet worse. For an only man he sure produces quite a few liquids. It must be the flesh that filters out the inner mushes.

I can feel my own flesh from the inside and it bothers me, but not as much as his. It's like he's constantly falling apart, leaving his person all over the place. I can't keep him together. Everywhere he goes. It wasn't always like this. I guess that's part of getting older.

When I met him, he was like a doll—self-contained and hollow. His flesh was smooth and when I touched it, it resisted me. Its elasticity would ensure its longevity, I thought. There seemed to be no way to puncture it. I tried a couple of times. When I saw him break through it, I thought he was faking. He was just trying to seem like everybody else—penetrable, full of red on the inside. I could see right through him, though, or rather, I couldn't. It was solid. When he drank something, it disappeared. It didn't disperse into the viscera. There was nothing in there, and yet, when he said that he loved me, I believed him.

I suppose that when you love something, it stays whole. But when you love something long enough, it starts to separate. Parts come away from other parts. Everything is imaginable apart, and there's no telling how it works back together. There's no way to get from one part to the other part without going through all of the stages of matter in between. The liquids and the solids and the gases that used to all be one amorphous and venerable thing come off like parts of garbage meat held together by a meat bucket slick with garbage broth.

"Do you want any of this bread?" he asks me.

"No," I say, "and I don't want you to eat it either."

He smiled, and I knew that I was joking after all.

When did I become so mindful of his inside parts?

November.

No, why?

Because the outside skins got in.

I suppose I never thought about how much of our material gets on the other on any given day. We wake up and trade face liquids, let our skin fall where it might and then go to bed again in a flesh broth. I try to wash it regularly but some of it must seep through, waiting inside the mattress for its chance to evolve and return, stronger than ever. I suppose we just get used to it, or we never think about it, or we try to imagine that the flesh is not so porous as all that, not as wasteful as all that, and certainly not as absorbent. We wear our flesh suits around and imagine that they will protect us from everything worse than us, and anything that helps the flesh suit stay strong must be taken internally. That's the only way to get to it, is from the inside. There aren't any starter holes to get through.

If you can feed the skin from the inside it will stay that way, through and through or rather, all around and everywhere. The openings close well enough or they're of use to it somehow. It too wears suits, artificial skins. Cotton replications of itself, or sometimes just the outer flesh of an animal corpse, there to serve its purpose but without a source of nutrients, it just falls away. Some parts of the flesh are hardier, and can be left exposed, while others are so delicate that they must never be. Most of the time, most of the flesh is kept inside a secondary skin suit.

He kept spilling his life all over the place, replacing bits as they fell off and leaking everywhere. For all of my complaints I envied him. He was a wellspring of fresh materials and always able to replicate. It was just as I cleaned one corner that a new one filled up, but he never lost anything of himself to it. It was always there for him, more and more, and he seemed to grow larger, despite how much of it he lost.

Meanwhile, my flesh reduced as would any corpse, and I could not eat the bread because it would rot within me. I had nothing left to mix it with, nothing to feed the snakes. The blood dries up because it has nowhere to go. Nothing comes in to water it down, and nothing gets out. Sometimes I seem to breathe, but the air that comes out is sour and well-worn. I was afraid of every puncture, as I knew that it would be the end of me. The holes would bring in air and swell up, condensing the surrounding flesh parts until I was mostly hole, with nothing to hold them together. Then he would be rid of me. But until then he is not.

BIOGRAPHIES

BLACK TELEPHONE
MAGAZINE
ISSUE 1

A

ALLISON, Shane

Shane Allison is the author of several poetry collections. His most recent being SWEET SWEAT from HYSTERICAL BOOKS. His visual art work can be seen @sdallison01 on IG

ARCHER, Azia

Azia Archer is a mother, writer, maker & lover living in Minnesota. She is the author of "Atoms & Evers" (dancing girl press, 2017. You can find her online at aziaarcher.com or via Twitter and Instagram @aziaarcher.

C

CALABY, Tara

Tara Calaby lives in Melbourne, Australia with her wife and far too many books. She is currently a PhD candidate in English, researching female patients in Victorian asylums. Calaby's writing has appeared in publications such as Galaxy's Edge,Grimdark MagazineandDaily Science Fiction. In her free time, she enjoys playing video games, reading comics and patting other people's dogs. Twitter @Tara_Calaby / Instagram as tara_calaby

CHAN, L

L Chan has been published at The Dark, Podcastle Magazine and Translunar Traveler's Lounge. He tweets @lchanwrites and maintains a site at lchanwrites.wordpress.com.

CHANG, Michael

MICHAEL CHANG (they/them) is the proud recipient of fellowships from Lambda Literary, Lighthouse Writers Workshop, Brooklyn Poets, & the Martha's Vineyard Institute of Creative Writing. Their writing has been published or is forthcoming in the Cincinnati Review, Summerset Review, Vassar Review, Minnesota Review, Santa Clara Review, Ninth Letter, Hobart, Harpur Palate, Poet Lore, & many others. Their collection <golden fleece> was a finalist for the Iowa Review Award in Poetry.

CHAPMAN, Clay

Clay McLeod Chapman writes books, children's books, comic books, film and TV. His most recent spooky novel is The Remaking (Quirk Books). Find him at www.claymcleodchapman.com.

CLEAVELAND, Kristin

Kristin Cleaveland has a Master's in English from Bowling Green State University and has worked as a professional writer, editor, and proofreader. She loves horror and dark fiction and has strong feelings about the Oxford comma. Find her on Twitter as @KristinCleaves.

D

DEBROT, Jacques

Jacques Debrot's stories have appeared or are forthcoming in many journals and anthologies, including Nothing Short of: Selected Tales from 100 Word Stories, The Rupture, Hobart, Fanzine, Maudlin House, and elsewhere. He has been nominated twice for a Pushcart Prize and won The Thorn Prize in Fiction and the Tusculum Review Fiction Prize.

E

EDENFIELD, Bryan

Bryan Edenfield was born in Arizona but has lived in Seattle since 2007. He was the founder and director of the small press and literary arts organization, Babel/Salvage. He hosted and curated the Glossophonic Showcase and the Ogopogo Performance Series. His writing has most recently been published in Sporklet, Mantra Review, Underwood Press, Meekling Review, TL;DR, and Plinth. He was a recipient of the Jack Straw Writers Fellowship for 2018 and is currently the host and producer of the Hollow Earth Radio program, Glossophonics.

ELSBY, Charlene

Charlene Elsby, Ph.D. is the Philosophy Program Director at Purdue University Fort Wayne and the author of Hexis and Affect. Facebook: charlene.elsby / Instagram: charlene_elsby / Twitter: @ElsbyCharlene

G

GREER, Maria

Born to an Argentinian mother and a bear-wrestling father, Maria Greer is a fiction writer, poet, and playwright based in Montana. Her work has appeared or is forthcoming in an eclectic variety of venues—print and online, fiction and nonfiction, academic and pop culture-focused. A map to them all can be found at mariagreer.com. She holds a degree in History and Creative Writing from Stanford University.

GRGAS, Lisa

Lisa's creative work has appeared in or is forthcoming from Tin House, The Literary Review, Adroit, K'in, Common Ground, Luna Luna, and Fractal. She lives in Hoboken, NJ.

H

HARPER, Elliot

Author of the dark science-fiction novella The City around the World published by Sinister Stoat Press, an imprint of Weasel Press, and the self-published speculative short story collection On Time Travel and Tardiness. My short fiction has appeared in FIVE:2:ONE Magazine's #thesideshow, Maudlin House, Queen Mobs Teahouse, the Ghost City Review, Akashic Book's #FriSciFi, Back Patio Press, Litro Magazine's #StorySunday, Dream Noir Lit Magazine, Vagabonds: Anthology of the Mad Ones Volume 8 and Riggwelter Journal. I regularly post short fiction and a blog on my website, elliotharper.com.

HUNTER, Victoria

Victoria Hunter is an awarded poet, from Pennsylvania, and has completed several writing courses. Her poem, "The Last Time, I Had To See You" was nominated for the 2020 Pushcart Prize. In Oct 2019, she was on the cover of Conceit Print Magazine. Two of her poems, are scheduled to appear on the blog called "Writing In A Woman's Voice." Her work has appeared in The Writers and Readers Magazine, Issues of Conceit Magazine, Sparks of Calliope Journal, Blue Hole Magazine, WordFest Anthology, and other press. She manages a YouTube channel, dedicated to the craft of poetry. YouTube: Poet Victoria Hunter
Blog:
writervictoriahunter.victoriahunter.net

J

JANESHEK, Jessie

Jessie Janeshek's full-length collections are MADCAP (Stalking Horse Press, 2019), The Shaky Phase (Stalking Horse Press, 2017), and Invisible Mink (Iris Press, 2010). Her chapbooks include Spanish Donkey/ Pear of Anguish (Grey Book Press, 2016), Rah-Rah Nostalgia (dancing girl press, 2016), Supernoir (Grey Book Press, 2017), Auto-Harlow (Shirt Pocket Press, 2018), and Channel U (Grey Book Press, forthcoming). Read more at jessiejaneshek.net. Instagram: @ fruitbatlashes / Twitter: @BlondeBitters

NEAL, Hannah

Beaux Neal (@hannahbolecter) is a musician, poet, and dancer in Atlanta, GA. Hit her @hannahbolecter on IG, Beaux Neal on Facebait.

PELAYO, Cynthia

Cynthia (Cina) Pelayo is the author of LOTERIA, SANTA MUERTE, THE MISSING, POEMS OF MY NIGHT, and the upcoming CHILDREN OF CHICAGO from Agora/Polis Books. Twitter: cinapelayo / Instagram: cinapelayoauthor

REYES, Dimitri

Dimitri Reyes is a Puerto Rican multidisciplinary artist, organizer, YouTuber, and Director of Marketing & Communications at CavanKerry Press. Hailing from Newark, New Jersey, he is the recipient of the SLICE Magazine's 2017 Bridging the Gap Award for Emerging Poets and a finalist for the 2017 Arcturus Poetry Prize by the Chicago Review of Books. Dimitri has organized and/ or performed with organizations such as Split this Rock, The Dodge Poetry Festival, The American Poetry Museum, Busboys & Poets, Rutgers University, and #PoetsforPuertoRico. He received his MFA from Rutgers University-

Newark and his poetry is published or forthcoming in Barely South, Duende, Vinyl, Entropy, Obsidian, Acentos, Kweli, and others.

Find him teaching poetry FOR FREE on YouTube
youtube.com/c/dimitrireyespoet
IG: @dimitri__reyes (two underscores)
FB: facebook.com/dimitri.reyes.507
Patreon: patreon.com/dimitrireyes

SINCLAIR, Robin

Robin Sinclair (they/them) is a queer, genderqueer writer of mixed heritage and mixed emotions, perpetually on the road, reading from their debut book of poetry, Letters To My Lover From Behind Asylum Walls (Cosmographia Books 2018). Robin's work has been published in various magazines and journals, including Across the Margin, Shot Glass Journal, Red Bird Chapbooks, The Cerurove, Yes Poetry, and Pidgeonholes. Find Robin at RobinSinclairBooks.com
Twitter: @Ghost_Of_Mary

SOPKIN, April

April Sopkin's work has appeared in Carve Magazine, Southern Indiana Review, The Southampton Review, failbetter, SAND Journal, and elsewhere. She lives in Richmond, Virginia. More info at aprilsopkin.com.

STEENEKAMP, Emelia

Emelia Steenekamp is a South African writer with a background in film-making, film scholarship, and digital art. They have been published or have work forthcoming in Misery Tourism, Strukturriss, Club Plum, The Gravity of the Thing and Datableed.

STONE, Crystal

Crystal Stone is an east coast girl with a Philly attitude. She is the author of three poetry collections Knock-Off Monarch (Dawn Valley 2018), All the Places I Wish I Died (CLASH 2021), and Gym Bras (Really Serious Literature 2021). Her work has previously appeared in The Threepenny Review, The Hopkins Review, Writers Resist, Salamander, Poetry Daily and many others. She is an MFA graduate from Iowa State University, where she gave a TEDx talk called "The Transformative Power of Poetry" in April 2018. You can find her at her website crystalbstone.com.

T

TEDESCO, Kailey

Kailey Tedesco is the author of She Used to be on a Milk Carton (April Gloaming Publishing) and Lizzie, Speak (winner of White Stag Publishing's 2018 MS contest). Her newest collection, FOREVERHAUS, will be released from White Stag in 2020. She is a senior editor for Luna Luna Magazine, and she teaches an ongoing course on the witch in literature at Moravian College. You can find her work featured or forthcoming in Black Warrior Review, Gigantic Sequins, Bone Bouquet Journal, Fairy Tale Review, and more. For further information, please follow @ kaileytedesco.

V

VALENTE, Stephanie

Stephanie Athena Valente lives in Brooklyn, NY. Her published works include Hotel Ghost, waiting for the end of the world, and Little Fang (Bottlecap Press, 2015-2019). She has work included in Reality Hands, TL;DR, and Cosmonauts Avenue. She is the associate editor at Yes, Poetry. Sometimes, she feels human. stephanievalente.com + @ stephanie.athena

W

WYTOVICH, Stephanie

Stephanie M. Wytovich is an American poet, novelist, and essayist. Her work has been showcased in numerous venues such as Weird Tales, Gutted: Beautiful Horror Stories, Fantastic Tales of Terror, Year's Best Hardcore Horror: Volume 2, The Best Horror of the Year: Volume 8, as well as many others.

Wytovich is the Poetry Editor for Raw Dog Screaming Press, an adjunct at Western Connecticut State University, Southern New Hampshire University, and Point Park University, and a mentor with Crystal Lake Publishing. She is a member of the Science Fiction Poetry Association, an active member of the Horror Writers Association, and a graduate of Seton Hill University's MFA program for Writing Popular Fiction. Her Bram Stoker Award-winning poetry collection, Brothel, earned a home with Raw Dog Screaming Press alongside Hysteria: A Collection of Madness, Mourning Jewelry, An Exorcism of Angels, Sheet Music to My Acoustic Nightmare, and most recently, The Apocalyptic Mannequin. Her debut novel, The Eighth, is published with Dark Regions Press.

Follow Wytovich on her blog at stephaniewytovich.blogspot.com/ twitter @SWytovich.

**PICK UP THE BLACK TELEPHONE
WE'RE LISTENING...**

THEMES

memory • love • death • spiritualism • loss

WE ACCEPT

poetry • short stories • essays

FOLLOW US

Twitter
@blacktelephonem

Instagram
@blacktelephonemagazine

Email
editorblacktelephonemag@gmail.com

Website
clashbooks.com